Edward Upward was born in 1903 at Romford, and was educated at Repton and at Corpus Christi College, Cambridge, where he read English and History, and was awarded the Chancellor's Medal for English Verse. While at Cambridge he created with Christopher Isherwood a series of stories about the fictitious village of Mortmere. After graduating he became a schoolmaster; from 1931 until his retirement in 1961 he taught at Alleyn's School, Dulwich, where he was a housemaster and head of the English department.

Edward Upward's first novel, *Journey to the Border*, was originally published by Leonard and Virginia Woolf at the Hogarth Press in 1938. In the 1930s he also contributed articles to *New Country*, *New Writing* and the *Left Review* and was on the editorial board of *The Ploughshare*, journal of the Teachers' Anti-War Movement. For sixteen years he was a member of the Communist Party of Great Britain, but he left it in 1948 because he believed it was ceasing to be a Marxist party.

Between 1942 and 1961 Upward wrote nothing, mainly for political reasons, but in 1962 Heinemann published *In the Thirties*, the first part of his trilogy of novels *The Spiral Ascent*. The second part, *The Rotten Elements*, and the third, *No Home but the Struggle*, were published in 1969 and 1977. Edward Upward's other books include *The Railway Accident and Other Stories* (1969), *The Night Walk and Other Stories* (1987), and in the current Enitharmon series, *The Mortmere Stories* and a revised version of *Journey to the Border*.

Since 1962 Edward Upward and his wife have lived at Sandown in the Isle of Wight. They have a son and a daughter and four grandsons.

EDWARD UPWARD
An Unmentionable Man

INTRODUCED BY FRANK KERMODE

London
ENITHARMON PRESS
1994

First published in 1994
by the Enitharmon Press
36 St George's Avenue
London N7 0HD

Distributed in Europe
by Password (Books) Ltd.
23 New Mount Street
Manchester, M4 4DE

Distributed in the USA
by Dufour Editions Inc.
PO Box 449, Chester Springs
Pennsylvania 19425

ISBN 1 870612 64 7 (paper)
ISBN 1 870612 79 5 (cloth edition,
limited to 25 copies, numbered and signed
by Edward Upward and Frank Kermode)

Set in 10pt Times by Bryan Williamson, Frome,
and printed by The Cromwell Press, Wiltshire

Contents

BOOKS BY EDWARD UPWARD

Journey to the Border (Hogarth Press, 1938)

*

THE SPIRAL ASCENT: A Trilogy
In the Thirties (Heinemann, 1962)
The Rotten Elements (Heinemann, 1969)
No Home but the Struggle (Heinemann, 1977)

The Spiral Ascent was also published in one
volume by Heinemann in 1977, and reissued in three
paperback volumes by Quartet in 1978-79.

*

The Railway Accident and Other Stories (Heinemann, 1969;
Penguin, 1972 and 1988)
The Night Walk and Other Stories (Heinemann, 1987)

*

Journey to the Border – a revised version (Enitharmon, 1994)
introduced by Stephen Spender

An Unmentionable Man (Enitharmon, 1994)
introduced by Frank Kermode

with Christopher Isherwood
The Mortmere Stories (Enitharmon, 1994)
introduced by Katherine Bucknell

Introduction

Readers of this collection of interlinked stories may well come to suspect that its title alludes to the long neglect suffered by its author – to the fact that his work is rarely mentioned because, for whatever reasons, controllers of critical opinion have decided that it should not be. The suspicion will not be far off the mark. And it is surely not unreasonable that Upward, in old age, and nearing the end of a writing career that has extended over more than sixty years, should make this neglect a part of his subject.

A remarkable story, 'The Procession', published seven years ago in *The Night Walk and Other Stories*, tells, in Upward's usual highly idiosyncratic manner – dreamlike narrative, yet precisely stated, part allegory, part fantasy – about an old artist who is watching what he takes to be his own funeral. A critic, once, long ago, a friend, accosts him and with condescending malice attributes the old man's lack of fame to his desertion of his earliest fantastic manner of writing, which, according to the critic, he abandoned in favour of the 'flat and unallusive naturalistic stuff you've confined yourself to for the last twenty-five years'. The artist (crudely, Upward in the disguise of a painter) offers his own explanation as to why he abandoned that admired manner: he felt that it was of the highest importance that his paintings should not ignore 'the real horrors of the contemporary world', or neglect the struggle to end them. Then he meets another old friend, a more famous painter, who is also reproachful, but for different reasons: he too regrets the abandonment of the early style, and thinks that if his friend, rather than rejecting it, had been able to combine it with his later, plainer manner he would have been a greater artist. Here were two explanations of his

7

neglect; but Upward, with a characteristically bold narrative swerve, ends the story by claiming that in fact he *has* done, without its being recognised, exactly as the painter wanted. Indeed the story itself demonstrates that he has done so; and he claims that 'after all' he has found a way to 'tell the truth about reality in a style that comes more readily to me than naturalism'.

One can think of no other author who could possibly have written 'The Procession', and the same may be said of all the stories in the present book. The earlier manner, the 'style that comes more readily', is, in its original form, exemplified by 'The Railway Accident', a much admired story of 1929, fantastic in a manner owing something to surrealism, and redolent of the Mortmere fantasies he devised at Cambridge with his friend Christopher Isherwood. (The character of Allen Chalmers, rebel and fantasist, in Isherwood's early book *Lions and Shadows*, is based on Upward, whose influence on the young Isherwood, and also on W.H. Auden, is part of the literary lore of the period.)

The apparent switch to a quite different style, a grey, flat style, often marked by a deliberate naiveté signifying a commitment to socialist realism, came with *In the Thirties*, published in 1962, as the first volume of the trilogy called *The Spiral Ascent*. Upward had left the British Communist Party in 1948, convinced that it had betrayed the ideals of Lenin, to which he himself remained devoted. Even as his old friends from the Thirties moved away from the Left and into well-paid jobs with free travel and expense accounts he was engaged in his own struggle, his effort to combine a deep commitment to the cause of the people with the vocation of artist. Many of his stories express the isolation to which this condemned him, and the sense of rejection, the pain and resentment caused by the snubs that patient merit of the unworthy takes. His art, as the deviant or corrupt fail to recognise, is deeply excogitated, appropriate to the practice of the serious writer in the latest phase of capitalism (exemplified, in his view, by the dangers of nuclear war) and possibly the only art that is not false and evasive.

He had, then, devised a manner compatible with his aspirations, which were to write as an artist about ordinary people and the political struggle made necessary by the condition of their lives. And that was the style the critics, real and imagined, objected to, judging that he had simply dropped out from art into doctrinaire politics. Its deliberate simplicity, its lack of irony and knowingness, certainly contrasts strangely with the flamboyance of the youthful work.

It was very difficult to find a publisher for the third volume of the trilogy, *No Home but the Struggle*, which eventually appeared in 1977, eight years after the second *(The Rotten Elements)* and fifteen after the first *(In the Thirties)*. *The Spiral Ascent* was dismissed, for example by Samuel Hynes, a well-known critic and authority on the Thirties, as 'arid, unimaginative and unreadable'; yet in a fashion appropriate to its length and complexity it shows the same blend of fantasy, autobiography and realism as the late stories. It is true that the first volume contains some deliberately flat and naive writing. Later, however, the author may have seen it as appropriate to the dialectical scheme of his whole novel to remember and exploit the 'style that comes more readily to him', the style, we may call it, of the hard-edged dream. As always he sought, and this time on a grand scale, to reconcile his socialist commitment with his artistic vocation, the necessary synthesis of these two inescapable obligations. *The Spiral Ascent* is an heroic attempt to achieve that synthesis, as well as to discuss in detail the difficulties of achieving it.

The themes of these very original new stories, despite the difference of scale, are very similar. Upward has continued to hold 'naive and completely out-of-date left wing views'; he has been a fervent supporter of C.N.D. and sees the crisis of capitalism as imminent rather than an illusion surviving from the time of his youth. He will place his hero-self in real or fantasised situations that make him seem gauche, demoded, even innocent, and in political discussion he will seem, to the unillusioned, the ordinarily knowing, simple-minded. He knows that his belief in the power of the people to destroy capitalist imperialism is, in the expensive restaurants and comfortable clubs of the successful, an unmentionable subject, not so much feared as hopelessly and distastefully out of fashion. His bitter fantasy of neglect, which happens to reflect the truth, sometimes includes, as in these stories, the notion of persecution, even of physical violence

9

against him. He even concedes something to the imputation of paranoia, yet finds it nevertheless to have a basis in reality, as indeed it sometimes does. And fantasy-reality is full of surprises, not all menacing or horrible; an old man, caught in the middle of a civil war, may be granted the delight of an encounter with an old love.

These new stories give strong support to the claim that their author is 'one of the very few left-wing imaginative writers of literary ability who have not betrayed their principles' – though the apparent immodesty of that remark is at once qualified by the narrator's deprecatory response to it. The dialogue I refer to is in 'A Ship in the Sky', perhaps the most remarkable of these skilfully inter-related tales, and one which fully demonstrates the uses of fantasy in the cause of a unique form of realism.

Reflecting on his achievements in a very long career, one cannot avoid thinking that Upward presents in his work a reliable record of an extraordinary period of history. His unique blending of important twentieth-century styles reminds us that the past, in art as well as in politics, still has lessons for the future. We should be grateful that a devoted artist has lived so intensely through so much. For he is most certainly an artist. He is a master at representing dream and fantasy as quite at home in a reality necessarily presented from a strongly political point of view. The relation between his two commitments may have changed; he may no longer believe, as he once did, that only Communism can produce great art. But he remains convinced that the artist cannot escape the world of political strife, that if he declines the commitment to that as well as to his art he will fail. His claim is that he has not, like so many of his old acquaintance, accepted that failure. More obliquely, he reminds us that we have still not fully understood the Thirties, that critical decade in politics and the arts, which tried to face the problems, to them terrible and urgent, which we comfortably push out of sight and out of mind. It may be that our neglect of Upward is a measure of a more general and perhaps more costly negligence.

FRANK KERMODE

An Unmentionable Man

The casualty was brought into the hospital some while after he was mugged. As a result of Government pressure on the local Health Authority to economise, the number of ambulances available had been drastically cut and there was a considerable delay before one of them arrived to pick the injured elderly man up from the pavement. The ambulance-men gave him what first aid they could, but when they delivered him to the hospital he was left without any treatment for nearly half an hour on a stretcher in the corridor where a junior nurse now and then took a look at him. Recently 'in the interests of efficiency' one of the wards had been closed down, so the overworked house surgeon, in order to free a bed for the present urgent case, had to select a patient to send home who was not too obviously unfit to go (and who if having to return within a day or two could be counted as a new admission, thereby helping the business-minded hospital manager to assert that the hospital could take in more patients at present than it had been able to before the closure of the un-economical ward).

The only injuries the house surgeon found, after as careful an examination as he had time for, were an apparently superficial grazing of the skin down one side of the face of the mugged man and a swelling just above his temple on the other side. He was unconscious and restless, moving his arms and legs about, and at intervals he spoke three words, always the same three, enunciated very unclearly. The house surgeon thought they might be, 'Where am I?'; and it was true that this man – who now believed that he was standing on the white esplanade of a vividly sunlit lakeside town he had never visited before, and that he was gazing up at snow-topped mountains across the blue water of the lake – did wonder what country he had arrived in.

An expensive-looking white motor cruiser on the lake drew up alongside the esplanade near to where he stood, and a casually yet fashionably dressed group of men and women, chatting and laughing, emerged from it to walk over towards a large café where green tables were shaded beneath a boldly striped awning. He became conscious that he too wanted something to eat, but he would have to find a café less extravagant to eat in than this one would certainly be. He began to stroll away from it along the esplanade. He was soon among other strollers who, he noticed, were most of them talking in other languages than English. None of the cafés he could see as he moved on, walking a little more quickly, looked inexpensive. He would probably have to leave the esplanade and go a little way into the town before he could find a cheaper one. But would they accept English money there? Then a panicking doubt whether he had any money on him at all brought him to a sharp stop in his walk. However, after a frantic search twice over of each of the pockets of his jacket he could think of, he found in a suddenly remembered inner pocket his soft leather wallet with quite a number of English banknotes inside. He was still shaking with relief when he saw coming directly towards him from among the strollers a formerly close friend of his – Peter Knightley.

Peter, for more than a few seconds after being greeted by him, stared unrecognisingly and warily at him, almost as though suspecting him of being a drug or brothel tout. Slowly, a look of recognition came up over Peter's face; and, at last, 'Stephen Highwood,' he was able to say, with a friendly smile. 'What are you doing here?'

'That's what I'm wondering,' Stephen said.

Peter seemed on the point of asking Stephen to explain this peculiar answer, and then checked himself. The suspicion may have come to him that Stephen wasn't being jocular but was perhaps suffering from some kind of psychiatric disorder, which might reveal itself more definitely later on as they continued talking.

'What would you say to our having lunch together?' Peter proposed.

'A good idea.'

'There's an excellent place quite near here.'

Peter led the way towards a café which Stephen soon recognised as the very one he had just avoided because of the likelihood of its being extravagantly expensive. But since there was no escape for him now he tried to quell his alarm by telling himself that he would almost certainly not have too little money in his wallet to pay his share of the bill.

He followed Peter into the awning-shaded outer part of the café where the green tables were. A waiter in a black tailed-suit with a bow tie came briskly towards them, bowed, showed them to one of the tables and drew back the chairs for them. Stephen felt helplessly trapped. The waiter momentarily disappeared, then reappeared holding two gilt-lettered menu carts, one of which he handed to Peter before handing the other to Stephen, who glanced through it quickly for the least extravagant items.

'Well, what would you fancy for a starter?', Peter asked, in an inviting way that made Stephen wonder whether Peter might intend to stand him a free lunch; but, to be on the safe side, he said he would have chilled tomato juice. Peter beckoned the waiter and ordered this for Stephen and an hors d'oeuvre for himself consisting of anchovies, olives and whatnot else, which when it was all brought to the table looked like a complete meal on its own. However, it did not prevent Peter from talking, nor did any of the subsequent courses he chose, all of them more substantial than those chosen by Stephen.

'So you're not sure why you're here?' Peter said with smiling curiosity.

Stephen had a quick inspiration: 'I suppose I'm here mainly because at my present age of eighty-nine I hadn't yet seen this place, and I felt that if I didn't see it now I might not ever. And the journey here by air is only a short one.'

Peter, after getting this explanation, no longer appeared to suspect that Stephen might be psychiatrically ill. With a change of tone he asked, 'Didn't you think of visiting first some of the interesting ancient towns of Eastern Europe that you haven't seen yet?'

There was a hint of amicable irony in Peter's voice which Stephen did not like. Peter was no doubt getting at him on the assumption that he had a better opinion of the post-war Eastern Block regimes than of those in the Capitalist West. Stephen, instead of answering, said: 'And what are you doing here, Peter?'

'I'm having a holiday; and combining it with looking for material I can use in an article I've been commissioned to write.'

'Are you writing anything now besides your articles for the Press?' Stephen asked, trying not so amicably to get at Peter who had once written poetry but who in spite of persistent efforts had been unable to continue writing any. Peter, however, did not appear to be in the least discomfited by Stephen's question.

'I am working on a book about us all,' he said. A fondness came into his voice, and a look overspreading his face seemed to have something of the same warm and vulnerable ingenuousness it had at times had in the years when Stephen and he were regarded as being in the same group of young left-wing nineteen-thirties writers. Peter has been the youngest of them all.

'Will you be mentioning me in it?'

'Why, of course,' Peter said, seeming very surprised and even a little hurt by this question.

For a moment Stephen thought of leaving it at that and changing the subject. But a resentment which for many years he had refrained from revealing to Peter welled up irresistibly in him now, and he said, 'I may not have read every article you've written or television talk you've given about the 'thirties, but I have read and heard more than a few, and there wasn't one of them that didn't completely ignore me.'

Peter looked put out for a moment; then he retorted, 'If I didn't mention you, it can only have been because I was writing about happenings that you weren't directly involved in – such as the Spanish Civil War.'

Not going to Spain, though the Party which Stephen was a member of had not expected him to go, was something he had always felt guilty about, and Peter intuitively knew this. Stephen did his best not to let his face show that Peter had succeeded in wounding him at all. 'You have written articles and given radio and television interviews which had nothing to do with Spain,' he said, 'but were about various 'thirties writers – with the exception always of myself.'

'The reason I avoided saying anything about you was that I didn't want to be unfriendly.'

Stephen gave him an uncomprehending look, and Peter went on, 'I could have told my readers how much I admired your skill as a writer, but I should also have felt bound to tell them how much I dislike the naïve and now completely out-of-date left-wing views that have always been so evident in your writings.'

Stephen, to avoid getting into a futile argument in defence of his politics, asked, 'What about the conventional Capitalist views you have reverted to as you have grown older. Are you happy with them now?'

'No, not *happy*. But what else is there?'

'There is Marxism, which you have rejected in spite of the fact that present day Capitalism is in just the kind of crisis that Marx so well understood and explained.'

Peter said nothing. He gave the impression that he would be bored by any further discussion of this subject. Stephen tried to goad him by saying, 'I wonder if you have ever thought of religion as a solution to your problem?'

'Never!' Peter said. He grinned. Suddenly this copiously white-haired broad-shouldered ruddy-faced man, who was only six years less old than Stephen himself, appeared to Stephen as someone he must not die unfriendly with. And he said to Peter, 'Whatever our differences, I do feel that few things could be more sordid and unseemly than for old friends like ourselves to quarrel in old age.'

'I'm glad to hear you say that. I have never intended to quarrel with you, and I shall always think of you with affection.' After a brief silence between them, Peter called to the waiter to bring him the bill. 'I'm sorry to be so sudden,' he said to Stephen, 'but I've just realised that if I sit here any longer I shall be late for an interview I'm to have with Herr Postler, the Mayor of this town.'

He paid the bill, and stood up. Stephen stood up too, and as they walked out of the café Stephen said, 'I'd like to pay for my part of the meal.'

'Of course not. It's all on my expense account.'

'Oh well, thanks very much all the same.'

'I'm so glad we met today,' Peter said. 'Unfortunately I'm booked on a plane back to England later this afternoon, but certainly we must meet again before too long.'

'Yes we must,' Stephen said, feeling far from certain about it.

Smilingly Peter turned from him, and with a brief confident goodbye wave of the hand he walked briskly off along the esplanade.

Stephen standing still, undecided what to do next, became aware of a young man with long blond hair who had come up from behind him and who spoke to him by name: 'Mr Highwood, I hope you won't think me impertinent, but I was sitting at the table next to yours in the café – you may well not have noticed me – and I couldn't help overhearing the conversation between you and Mr Knightley. I found it extremely interesting.' Stephen looked at him with distrust, and asked, 'How do you know my name?'

'I deduced it from the conversation.'

Stephen didn't try to prevent his face from showing that this failed to make him any less distrustful, but the young man went on undeterred, 'I am a lecturer at a Yorkshire Polytechnic which has just become a University' – he smiled – 'and I am collecting material for a book I have been given the go-ahead to write, which is to be about the touristic, banking, religious, literary, artistic and scientific assocations of this town.'

'That seems rather a tall order,' Stephen said, interrupting him.

The young man laughed. 'It is,' he agreed. 'And I would be most grateful if you could help me by sparing a little of your time to give me your impressions of the place.'

'I've only just arrived here this morning. My impressions would be useless to anyone intending to produce a serious scholarly work.'

The young man ignored the unpromising tone of this. He continued, 'I could act as your guide. I have been here long enough to explore a number of the back streets as well as taking a look into most of the sumptuous hotels and other buildings open to the public along the esplanade.'

'Are you some kind of high-class tout?'

The young man did not take offence. 'No,' he said. 'I am an admirer – and have been for a long time – of your writing. And I would greatly value even your first impressions.'

'Which books of mine have you read?' Stephen challengingly asked.

'Every one of them that I could get hold of.'

Stephen was painfully reminded that all his books were out of print, and nearly all of them unobtainable in the majority of public libraries, but he was convinced now that the young man's admiration was sincere, and he was grateful to him for it.

'I'm sorry to have been so suspicious,' Stephen said to him.

'It's very understandable that you were,' the young man excusingly said.

'What is your name, by the way?' Stephen asked.

'Paul Irlam. I'm afraid I was more than a bit impertinent when I, a complete stranger to you, introduced myself by saying I had found your conversation with Peter Knightley extremely interesting.'

'Never mind,' Stephen said with a smile. 'But I'm curious to know what there was in it to interest you so much.'

'Several things; especially the fact that neither of the two reasons Knightley gave you, when he was trying to justify his never having mentioned you in his occasional articles and television interviews about the 'thirties, was the true one – though just possibly he may not have been conscious of this.'

'Well, what do you think was the true reason?' Stephen asked.

'He wasn't willing to go against the dominant opinion in Establishment circles now that it simply "isn't done" to mention you at all,' Paul Irlam said. 'There was a time when it would have been quite in order to refer to your work dismissively or disapprovingly, but that time has passed. They've decided now that you are to be obliterated – permanently.'

'You may be right,' Stephen agreed.

'I'm not suggesting that guidelines about you and certain other politically undesirable writers are passed down to loyal subordinates by a few topmost people meeting in the Carlton Club,' Paul Irlam said, 'but somehow it becomes generally understood that such writers are as far as possible to become non-existent.'

'I don't doubt that the people who would like to obliterate me would like even more to obliterate the political ideas I have supported in my writings.'

'They won't succeed in that,' Paul said. 'And your work has other admirers besides myself who are just as determined as I am to ensure that it isn't forgotten.'

'I'm happy to hear that,' Stephen said, 'and I shall always be grateful to you all; but I know that you have the economic crisis against you, and there is the probability of a devastating war which you and I will rightly regard as immeasurably more important than any writings of mine.'

'That's not the sort of talk that should come from a Marxist,' Paul said reprovingly. 'We shall never win if we don't confidently expect we can. But you must be a little tired after your journey. Would you be willing to go with me now to the inexpensive hotel I've found for myself in a back street? I'm sure they'll have a room for you, and the hotel isn't a bordel.'

'Thanks, yes. I would be glad to rest for an hour or two.'

They started at once to walk to the hotel.

It was a small one in a narrow street not far from the traffic-infested surroundings of a railway terminus, and it was clean besides being cheap. Stephen's room there had a bed covered with a duvet which – though he'd never found duvets easy to sleep under – he was now soon able to doze comfortably on top of without undressing.

When Paul woke him by knocking on his door, and came into the room to ask whether he felt ready to go to a place where they could eat which was very different from the café they'd both been in that morning, Stephen said he felt thoroughly rested and would be glad to go.

'First we shall have to traverse the red light district,' Paul said as they came out of the hotel on to the street. 'You'd better firmly hold your hat on there or you'll risk having it snatched from your head.'

The upper windows of a number of the houses in the district were wide open displaying a well illuminated woman sitting inside, and the street doors too were open, but no pimp tried to snatch Stephen's hat and run upstairs with it.

'Have you ever in your long life been up to one of the women in a district like this?' Paul asked.

'No.'

'Not even for the sake of an experience which could be useful to you as a writer?'

'No.'

'Why not?'

'Much too dangerous,' Stephen said.

They both laughed.

Quite soon Paul said, 'And here, just at the end of the street, is the restaurant we are going to eat in.'

'One thing I've been meaning to ask you,' Stephen said. 'Will they accept English bank notes?'

'You needn't worry,' Paul said. 'I'll be paying in the local currency for your share of the meal and you can recoup me in your money afterwards.'

'Thanks.'

'It's when we reach the places I'd like to take you to later this evening that you will need to worry about your money – and to keep a tight hold on it too.'

The restaurant was small and comfortable, and the waiter, who recognised Paul, was friendly. For their first course both Stephen and Paul chose artichokes of the thistle-like type with soft parts which are very edible when dipped in melted butter. The waiter, before going off to place their orders with the chef for the artichokes and the other courses they'd chosen, brought to their table a basket full of brioche rolls and a large carafe of red wine.

'This stuff seems remarkably strong,' Stephen commented after drinking less than a quarter of a glass.

'It is,' Paul said.

'And I should guess its quality is pretty good.'

'I'm sure it is,' Paul said. 'But don't let your liking for it be lessened by any fears that we're going to have a huge bill to pay. This restaurant is almost unbelievably modest in its charges.'

At the end of the meal the amount that Stephen and Paul had to pay was as modest as Paul had said it would be, considering the quantity as well as the quality of what he and Irlam had eaten and drunk. But after they went out from the restaurant into the open air Stephen felt very unsteady. As an old man he had become gradually less keen on alcoholic drinking, and when he did have a drink with friends it was never anything like as much as he'd had this evening. He decided to try not to let his inner unsteadiness become an outward staggering that Paul would notice; and in fact Paul did not seem to guess how Stephen felt.

'Now we'll visit the Arts Quarter,' he said.

'You told me earlier on that after our meal we would be going somewhere where I would need to keep a tight hold on my money,' Stephen said. 'Did you mean the Arts Quarter?'

'Yes, I did. But, apart from pickpockets and a few other more sinister characters including drug-peddlers, not everyone in the Quarter is simply out to fleece the tourists. I'll take you to two of the studios where we shall be able to look around and to talk to artists who won't press us to buy anything.'

'Do you think we shall see anything I might want to buy?'

'I doubt it,' Paul said. 'Certainly not from the first studio we're on our way to visit now; but I think I can promise you that you'll find it interesting.'

They didn't have to walk far. Paul came to a stop at one of the gaps in the railings that stretched along the front of a terrace of perhaps once fashionable though now decaying homes. 'The studio is down these steps here,' he told Stephen. 'Be very careful how you go. The street lamp above us is appallingly dim.'

They descended slowly to a rubbish-cluttered basement area which looked like the backside of a sleazy hotel. At the far end there was an open door from which light shone and a smell issued that was sweetly fragrant yet at the same time malodorous.

'Is this a studio?' Stephen asked.

Paul pointed to a cursively written brown inscription on white-painted plaster above the open doorway.

Stephen read the words, *THE EXCREMENTALISTS*.

'This is the "manufacturing" outer part of the studio,' Paul said quietly as they paused before going in through the doorway. 'The workers here call themselves "practical artists". The main part where the actual paintings are done is separated from this by double-doors. It can be reached also by steps going down to the next – and much less dirty – basement area farther along the street. That is the entrance used by nearly all the tourists who visit the studio. They are eager to see the famous/notorious painters at work in the main part of the studio; but few of them ask to see the "practical artists" at work in the outer part of it.'

'What exactly is manufactured here in the outer part?' Stephen asked.

'The peculiar material required by the "painter artists",' Paul answered. 'The "practical artists" create this from raw human excrement, some of which they themselves provide – though help from paid outside volunteers is needed to top it up. Of course it has to be deodorised and otherwise processed before it's fit to be conveyed through the double doors to the painters. But we'd better not hover here outside any longer, as one of the practicals might spot us and become suspicious. Or,' Paul quickly added, 'would you perhaps rather visit somewhere less disgusting?'

'Oh no,' Stephen said. 'What you've told me has made me extremely curious about these Excrementalists.'

He and Paul were noticed as soon as they entered the studio. A bulky youngish man in a dark brown overall came towards them, staring with undisguised suspicion at Stephen.

'He's all right, Crags,' Paul said, evidently on good enough terms with the man to call him without offence by what Stephen thought likely to be his nickname. 'My friend Mr Stephen Highwood isn't a police spy. He is a distinguished writer, and he's very keen to be shown over both parts of this unique studio.'

'How do,' Crags said, and Stephen was fastidiously relieved that he didn't offer to shake hands.

On the centre of the concrete floor in this 'practical' part of the studio were two large upright corrugated metal cylinders with a wooden bung near the bottom of each. A man who wore the same kind of brown overall as Crags did was standing beside one of the cylinders.

'Jock,' Crags called out to him, 'we've a visitor with Mr Irlam here wanting to see how the process works.'

Jock glanced only briefly at Stephen, nodded recognisingly to Paul, then bent down and released the bung from the cylinder.

A slurry of excrement flowed thickly out into a capacious flat metal tray below it, and as it did so he turned on a brass tap which sprayed the flow with a scent so powerful that Stephen momentarily had difficulty in restraining himself from vomiting.

When the tray was filled almost to the brim Jock replaced the bung. Next he stepped back from the cylinder and went to pull a small lever among the dials of a black panel fixed against the wall. Crags, without needing to be asked by Stephen, readily explained this latest stage of the process. 'The lever controls the heating of the slurry,' he said. 'The liquidness has to be lessened, but the slurry must not be baked. It must be soft, and its softness has to be of a kind that will allow the painters to apply it to their canvases with a small trowel, or with a brush if they soften it further by adding oil to it. And it must be capable of retaining any colour they choose to give it.'

Stephen, thinking he detected a note of jealousy in the way that Crags spoke of the painters, dared to ask him, 'What is there for you in this work you are doing?'

Crags did not take offence. 'Well,' he said, 'I won't pretend that I'm not attracted by the pay I'm getting here, which is far better than I'd get for any equally mucky job elsewhere, and many "clean" white-collar office workers are paid far worse. Also, since my prospering employers in the painters' part of the studio know that I do my job here pretty efficiently, I can feel quite secure in it.'

At this point Jock abruptly showed that while regulating the heating of the slurry he had been listening to Stephen and Crags. 'There's much more for me in the work I do here than that,' he said. 'I have the same views about the world as the painters have who founded this studio, and I think of myself as a practical *artist* without whose basic help they would be unable to create paintings which embody these views.' He turned to Stephen, and he added, 'But you must talk with the painters themselves. They can explain these things to you from first hand experience.'

'Thank you very much,' Stephen said.

'He's a philosopher, our Jock is,' Crags jokily told Stephen, 'and he speaks like one.'

Paul said, 'Well, thank you both very much for telling us about your work, and now I think we should leave you to it and take a look at the inner part of the studio.'

He led Stephen to the double doors, and surprised him by saying, 'Go in ahead of me.' Stephen pushed open the first door, which was handleless and had a covering of red baize. He found himself in a space that would have been completely dark if some of the light from the outer studio hadn't followed him into it while Paul still held the door open behind him. Stephen tried to push open the second door but failed, even though he pushed hard. When Paul closed the first door and he and Stephen were in complete darkness, there was a startlingly loud whirring sound just above their heads.

'What's that?' Stephen asked.

'That's an electric extractor,' Paul said, 'which is automatically started up by the shutting of the first door and removes all the smells of the manufacturing studio from the air in here.'

After a minute or two the noise abruptly stopped. 'Now I shall push the second door and you'll see that it will open with ease,' he said. 'The doors are controlled by a clever device which ensures that they can never be open at the same time and that both remain shut for as long as the extractor is still switched on.'

He opened the second door, which appeared to be made of heavy oak, and it closed behind them automatically when they stepped out into the artists' studio. Stephen had an impression of many people moving about, some pausing to watch the artists painting at their easels, others gazing at the various framed canvases, large and small, hanging numerously on the studio walls. No one seemed to notice Paul and Stephen for a while, until suddenly a young woman detached herself from the crowd and came straight towards them. She welcomingly recognised Paul; but like Crags before her, though much less crudely, she showed an unmistakable suspiciousness of Stephen. Paul, however, was quickly able to dispel this when he introduced him to her.

'Kirsty,' he said to her, 'this is my friend Stephen Highwood, the distinguished writer. He is eager to see the work of the painters here.'

She was honest enough not to pretend she had heard of him

23

before, but her smile told him she was glad that he wanted to see the paintings.

He became conscious that she had an extraordinarily beautiful face.

'We have to be very watchful,' she said, in an apologetic tone which confessed that she had been unjustly suspicious of him. 'We do get the occasional police officer in disguise who is reconnoitring in preparation for a raid by the vice squad. Several of our painters and even a visitor or two have been arrested before now and have been quite brutally interrogated in police cells, though all of them so far have been released without any charge being brought against them. The fact is that the authorities in this world-known town are very reluctant to risk putting visitors off by appearing to have intolerantly old-fashioned views about modern art. But let us go and see the canvases now on display so that you' – she spoke to Stephen, not Paul – 'can form your own opinion of them.' (Presumably she already knew Paul's opinion.) 'We won't interrupt the artists at their work, unless of course you want to buy one of their paintings.'

'Are you yourself a painter, by the way?' Stephen asked.

'No. My job is simply to look after the visitors and to answer their questions. But I am very much in sympathy with the outlook which led these artists to found this studio.'

'What sort of outlook is that?' Stephen asked.

'A loathing for the whole anti-human ideology of the murderous present-day powers who rule the world,' she said.

'You make me even more eager than I already was to see these paintings,' he said, genuinely and not just to please her – though he felt a growing desire to please her.

Paul, aware that Stephen was attracted by her, tactfully took no part in his further talk with her after she had guided them through the crowd of visitors towards one of the larger framed canvases hanging from the wall.

'This is by Bradnock,' she said. 'It is his own favourite, and he has priced it so highly that perhaps he doesn't really want to part with it. But I suspect that some millionaire is bound to turn up sooner or later who will not hesitate to pay almost any price Bradnock may ask for it. What do you think of it?'

Stephen's first impression was of a great variety of colours heavily applied to the canvas, perhaps with a small trowel such as Crags had mentioned, and only after a while did he realise that the painting was representational. It exhibited a pinkish-fleshed human female rump across which, and also across the widely parted white thighs below it, there were deeply red raised lines such as could have been caused by a whip.

'Well, how do you like this?' Kirsty asked.

'Is the painter some kind of pathological pervert?' Stephen asked, aware of using an old-fashioned word.

'Not at all,' she said. 'He's perfectly "normal", and quite sane.'

'Does that mean he's just a pornographer cynically out to make money?'

'Of course not,' she said a little sharply. 'I've told you before that what unites all the artists here is a loathing of the world's criminal rulers.'

'Yes,' he said, 'but I can't see how these artists can claim to be attacking our rulers by producing paintings like this one.'

'They regard themselves as "super-subversionists",' she said. 'They believe that the visual images they create with excremental paint can significantly contribute to the already far-gone corruption of the present social and economic system, and can help to accelerate its final self-destruction.'

'I wouldn't rely on corruption, however ingeniously it may be deepened by Excremental artists, to break the power of our rulers over us,' Stephen said. 'That power needs to be forcibly overthrown by the working class.'

'To my admittedly disillusioned mind this seems a somewhat outdated notion,' Kirsty said.

'I agree with Stephen,' Paul said.

'Well,' she said, 'I wonder how Stephen will like the paintings in the studio of The Resuscitationists, if that's where you're taking him next?'

'Yes, I am.'

'Please don't feel I'm not grateful for the time you've given to explaining so clearly what the Excrementalists are aiming at,' Stephen said anxiously.

Kirsty gave him a nice smile. Then he asked, 'Could you tell me what you think of these Resuscitationist artists? We unfortunately shan't have you as a guide when we get to their studio.'

'They aim to revive the idea that true Art is never *about* anything in the external world, and especially never about politics. They consider that the Excrementalists are politically motivated, and they despise them. They argue that Art is a world in its own right.'

Kirsty would have continued, but at this instant a squad of stout leather-belted black-uniformed policemen, with handgun holsters attached to their belts, abruptly invaded the studio. Arbitrarily it seemed, they seized hold of a number of the visitors, including, to Stephen's horror, his new friend Paul. But Paul though roughly handled was able, before the policeman who held him could clap a hand over his mouth, to shout to Stephen, 'Get away quick!' And Stephen did get away, running as quickly as at his age he could towards the same door by which the police had entered the studio (he knew it would have been futile for him to try to get through the double doors that led into the outer studio); and, strangely, a solitary policeman who had been left behind on guard at the entrance made no attempt to prevent him from escaping.

There was something strange also about the street he found himself in when he got outside. It was very narrow, quite unlike the street he had walked along to the Excrementalists' 'manufacturing' studio earlier in the evening with Paul. Stranger still was its name, Town Lane, which he suddenly saw on an oblong enamel plate attached to the windowless wall of a small house. A moment later he realised he was in deadly danger. Two young men wearing identical tee-shirts which had the word BRITISH inscribed in crimson lettering across them, and identical dark blue shorts with union jacks vividly printed on them, were advancing menacingly towards him, and he knew he could have no hope of escape from them.

*   *   *   *   *

26

The hospital had at last contacted his wife, and she was standing at his bedside with the house surgeon now. Stephen's eyes were both partly open, and she had the feeling that he recognised her. Also he was saying something, but it was incoherent and unintelligible to her.

'He has been like this ever since he was brought in here,' the house surgeon said.

'But I do feel that he recognises me,' she said.

The house surgeon, looking at her with a compassion which was genuine enough, said, 'He may well recognise you, though I am afraid we must face up to the possibility that he may never make a full recovery.' He had a momentary impulse to add, 'The kindest thing that could happen to your husband might be to die now.' However, his conscience warned him that such a suggestion, besides being cruel to her, would be tainted by an irritable regret that he would not be able to tell the hospital manager that the old man's bed would be free for the next patient; so he went on to say to her, 'But he looks strong for his age, and it is not at all impossible that he could almost fully recover. I shall do the very best I can for him.'

The house surgeon, as she said goodbye and told him she would be coming to the hospital again on the following day, noticed tears in her eyes. Yet he could not refrain from saying, 'I hope you will not mind my asking if you know what made your husband go out alone at this time of night in this town where so many muggings are taking place.'

'Yes, I do know,' she said. 'It must have been due to one of those attacks of fury that sometimes came over him about the way his writing was being ignored, and whenever they came he just had to go out and pace the streets.'

The Unmentionable Thing

The condition of the elderly writer, Stephen Highwood, had shown no improvement since he was brought into hospital on the previous evening after being mugged in town. When his wife was at last contacted then, she saw him moving his limbs about restlessly under the sheets of a bed provided with cot sides as a precaution against his throwing himself out. He seemed to be saying something, though incoherently, and his eyes were half open. They were still half open now that she was seeing him on the following day, and he was still trying to say something. Once again with tears in her eyes she told the house surgeon she was convinced that Stephen recognised her, and once again the house surgeon hadn't the heart to cast doubt on this. But he was glad to be able to tell her truthfully that he thought her husband's speech was clearer than it had been the first time. At least two of the words among several others he'd spoken today had been very distinct. The words were, 'the Pavilion'. Did these mean anything to her? She answered that unfortunately they did not.

Stephen believed himself to be on his way now to a well-known Pavilion in one of the public parks of a great metropolis. He had arranged to meet his old friend Peter Knightley outside the Pavilion, but he was having difficulty in finding it. He had never been here before, and he felt as though bewitched and disoriented by the extraordinary trees that fringed the extensive lawn-like central space of the park. The only one of these that he recognised – and he was pleased with himself for remembering the name of such a rare one – was a Service-Tree of Fontainebleau. Then, after uncertainly walking on for a while, he quite abruptly came upon the Pavilion, and saw Peter Knightley standing outside it.

Peter's reason for choosing this rendezvous had been that Stephen would more easily locate it than the nearby exclusive Club called The Elzevir where he was to be introduced to Peter's fellow clubman Sir Barnard Musgrave, the publisher, who had invited him to lunch there.

The Club was at the end of a cul-de-sac among confusingly numerous other imposing metropolitan buildings, and during their somewhat complicated short walk to reach it Peter had time to add a few more details to those he'd already given Stephen about the kind of man Sir Barnard was.

'He calls himself a Tory Anarchist, which does not amuse his fellow members of the Conservative Party, though he is using the word "anarchist" not in a Kropotkin sense but merely to mean that he wants Government interference in the business affairs of private citizens to be reduced to a minimum. You'd have thought that most Tories wouldn't have taken exception to this at all, but I suppose there must be something about him personally that gets their goat. Perhaps it's the fact that he boasts about being more liberal than the Liberals, and more tolerant of socialism than the Labour Party.'

'What have you told him about me?', Stephen asked.

'I've let him know of your difficulty in getting anything published nowadays, and I've praised the literary quality of your writing.'

'Did you touch on the subject of my being a left-winger?'

'Yes, of course. But that didn't seem to put him off at all.'

Stephen was unable to question Peter any further because they had now reached the front doorway of the Club at the end of the cul-de-sac. The door was a single one with a semi-circular Georgian fanlight above it and austerely undecorated square white pillars on either side of it. Stephen managed to overcome a feeling of intimidation which for a moment arose in him as Peter, without having to use a key or ring a bell, opened the door and signed to him to go in first.

No one came forward to check up on their right to enter the Club. The informality of this caused a slight uneasiness in Stephen, which was augmented a moment later by the impression of luxury he got from the sight overhead, in the quite small though high entrance hall, of a large gilded chandelier with numerous unlit electric candles shinily whitened by the mid-morning daylight shafting through a tall and narrow window; and his uneasiness was not lessened when Peter led him into a bigger room where the wallpaper was designed to resemble tapestry and had hunting scenes depicted on it. Only a few clubmen – no women were present – sat in the chairs here, which were upholstered in plush of the same deep red colour as the jackets of the huntsmen pictured on the wallpaper. Soon from one of these chairs Sir Barnard, a middle-aged man who wore a well-tailored suit and had a round open-looking face, rather slowly stood up.

Peter introduced Stephen to him. Sir Barnard, perhaps suspecting that Stephen might need putting at his ease, or perhaps merely because he himself might be a keen drinker wanting a drink, said with a smile, 'I suggest we start off by having an immediate pre-prandial aperitif. I can very strongly recommend the Club's French Vermouth. And you'll have one too,' he added to Peter, 'though you've told me you won't be able to stay to lunch.'

'I'm sorry to say you will have to include me out even from the aperitif,' Peter said, 'I'm already overdue to attend a buffet lunch at the Press Club to which our President, very much on his own initiative, has invited a certain Cabinet Minister who I think may be no favourite of yours.'

'I believe I can guess who you mean,' Sir Barnard said. 'Good luck to you. Grill him thoroughly, and tell me about it later.'

As soon as Peter had left them Sir Barnard signalled to Stephen to sit down in a red plush armchair beside him. He beckoned to a young waiter, who wore a huntsman's red jacket, and ordered two large French Vermouths; then turned to Stephen and said, 'The first time I came across anything written by you was when I was a schoolboy aged fourteen.'

Stephen was startled to be reminded that he was nearly forty years senior to this prestigious publisher he had been regarding almost as a superior elder.

'The circumstances were quite peculiar,' Sir Barnard went on.

'I was a fag then at a well-known public school' – he named it, but Stephen whose hearing nowadays was less acute than in his younger years did not catch the name – 'and the lavatories in the yard of the House I belonged to were a bit primitive. They were earth closets. When you'd done your business you pressed down a lever and a fixed quantity of earth was released on to it from a large wooden box which was placed where the cistern would have been in a civilised water closet.'

The red-jacketed young waiter arrived at this point with the two large glasses of Vermouth on a silver tray, which looked as if it might be an antique. Well-trained, he held out the tray for Stephen, Sir Barnard's guest, to be the first to take one of the glasses.

After the waiter had gone from their table Sir Barnard raised his glass to Stephen and Stephen raised his glass to Sir Barnard. Stephen couldn't help having an optimistic feeling that Sir Barnard might already, on Peter's recommendation, be intending to publish some of his recent work, perhaps even before seeing any of it. They drank to each other in silence.

Sir Barnard remained silent for some while after this, and Stephen began to hope he was going to drop the subject of the earth closets and to get on to talking now about his publishing intentions. But he didn't.

Having finished his Vermouth, he said, 'The earth-covered excrement of the forty or so boys in the House was not wasted. Forgive me for digressing like this but I just can't resist it. One of the youthful remembrances that will come to me every now and then for the rest of my life is the sight of the vegetable-growing plot of ground where the enriched earth was spread for manure. The ground was quite near the House, and every boy of us (or perhaps I should say "man", which was our customary appellation for one another at this school) knew about the provenance of the manure, because used toilet paper was often visible in it. But that's enough of that. Let us go and have lunch, and I'll tell you then how I came upon that first piece of writing by you which I admired so much.'

Stephen waited for Sir Barnard to lift himself, rather slowly again, from his armchair; then was reminded of his own greater age by not being able to stand up any less slowly. Sir Barnard led him out of the sitting-room, with its tapestry-resembling hunt-depicting wallpaper and its red-jacketed waiters, into a dining-room that was even larger and contained real palm trees growing from big brass-bound mahogany tubs alongside walls which had three contrasting colours painted in horizontal bands on their smoothly plastered surfaces. The band nearest to the dining-room floor was pale brown, the next above it was deep blue and the highest, reaching the ceiling, was light blue. Stephen realised that the lowest was meant to represent sand, while the middle and top bands represented sea and sky respectively. And on the sand were half-sized human figures sunbathing, male and female, some of the females wearing nothing but bikinis.

The dining-room walls had no windows. All the light came from an arched sunlight-coloured glass skylight high overhead which roofed the whole length of the dining-room. For evening dinner presumably the skylight would have to glow with electrically imitated sunshine.

A waiter in a white jacket with black trousers and a black bow-tie – no doubt this was part of the Mediterranean effect that seemed to be aimed at in the dining-room – came to lead Sir Barnard, followed by Stephen, to the table that had been reserved for him. Another waiter appeared immediately afterwards with two menus.

'What would you like for your hors-d'oeuvre?' Sir Barnard asked Stephen.

'I think I would like creamed mushrooms,' he said.

'I will have the chilled pineapple juice,' Sir Barnard told the waiter. 'And we may as well decide now what we want for our main course.'

Once again Stephen was in doubt, but not wanting to linger too long he said, 'I'll choose the cheese and asparagus pancakes.'

'I'm sure they will be very good,' Sir Barnard said. 'Are you a vegetarian, perhaps?'

'Only as often as I can be.'

But Sir Barnard did not trouble to ask what Stephen meant by this. 'Ptarmigan for me,' he told the waiter. 'And you might send someone with the wine list to us.'

As soon as the waiter had left them Sir Barnard said, 'Now I'll tell you how at the age of fourteen I found the first piece of writing by you that I had ever read.'

He was interrupted by a different waiter, who hastened to them with a wine list. 'Haven't you got two of these?' Sir Barnard asked with more than a hint of displeasure in his voice.

The wine waiter was about to hurry off to fetch a second list when Stephen said to Sir Barnard, 'Please choose for me. I can't pretend to be knowledgeable about wines.' He gave the waiter a quick side-glance of sympathy, which the waiter however avoided appearing to notice. 'Well,' Sir Barnard said, 'I'll choose the Club's Crozes-Hermitage. I think you'll like it.' Then he turned to the waiter: 'And with the sweet course we will have the Club's White Burgundy.' The waiter took the wine list, bowed to Sir Barnard, and without a glance at Stephen, he left them.

Sir Barnard managed to continue talking while he sipped the chilled pineapple juice which the first waiter, who had already brought the creamed mushrooms for Stephen, now placed before him on the table.

'From the floor of the outbuilding where the earth closets were,' Sir Barnard then said to Stephen, 'I picked up one morning a sheet of paper on which had been handwritten very neatly a copy of the beginning of your prose poem *The Mainland*. It immediately appealed very much to me. I supposed that the copy had been accidentally dropped by someone in our House, but I couldn't for the moment think of anyone in the House who would have been likely to make such a copy. I dropped it again in case he might come back to look for it here. And the next time I visited the outbuilding the sheet of paper had gone.'

Sir Barnard allowed himself to be interrupted by the arrival at their table of the wine waiter carrying a bottle of the Club's Crozes-Hermitage. Using a white napkin to hold the bottle by its neck the waiter expertly tipped a small quantity of the wine into Sir Barnard's glass, and Sir Barnard tasted it with a serious care which convinced Stephen that he was a genuine connoisseur. The waiter than poured the wine into Stephen's glass before pouring it into Sir Barnard's.

After he had left their table another waiter came to remove Sir Barnard's chilled pineapple juice glass and Stephen's creamed mushrooms plate, and almost immediately afterwards a third waiter arrived with the Ptarmigan and with the cheese and asparagus pancakes.

Sir Barnard continued talking during the main course just as he had while sipping the pineapple juice.

'Since the day I found that sheet of paper,' he said, 'I think I've read almost everything of yours which has been published. Later on, after I became a publisher I could have kicked myself for not having become one before Pringle and Petit got you on their list. But now it seems that neither they nor any other publisher you have so far tried will publish what you write. Why is this?'

'It's because in my writings I make a point of mentioning unmentionable things.'

'Unmentionable things!' Sir Barnard loudly exclaimed. 'I should have thought that since the prosecution failed against that atrociously written book by D.H. Lawrence about a game-keeper, nothing is unmentionable, and personally I am heartily glad of it.'

'I know that if I wrote stories about things such as geronto-philism in Ashby-de-la-Zouch, to take a very unlikely example just for the sound of the word "Zouch", I wouldn't be found guilty of mentioning the unmentionable. But,' and now Stephen felt a rising anger he was unable to prevent from making itself heard in his voice, 'I don't write pornography. I write to expose the root cause of the horrific sufferings of so many millions of our fellow human beings in the present-day world. I accuse the imperialistic capitalist system. I give warning that this system, if allowed to go on much longer, could destroy not merely more than half the human race but quite possibly the whole of it. However, I still haven't told you the truly unmentionable and most important thing I've mentioned in my writings.'

'And what might that be, I wonder.'

Sir Barnard's tone was lightly sarcastic. And there was a smile on his face which slowly disappeared as Stephen went on, 'The truly unmentionable thing I've mentioned is that the peoples of the world, if only they can realise soon enough that it is in their interests to support one another internationally – and I'm sufficiently optimistic to believe they will – are capable of overthrowing imperialism and of beginning to create a world in which most of the human race will be happier than they have ever been before.'

'Of course, although I totally disagree with all this Utopian nonsense –,' Sir Barnard began, but Stephen quite passionately interrupted him.

'I am not a Utopian,' Stephen said; 'I'm well aware that there will never be a heaven on earth, or anywhere else for that matter.'

Sir Barnard ignored Stephen's interruption and went on, 'I was going to say that although disagreeing entirely with your views I have every intention of publishing you. But we are likely to be faced with a little difficulty, at present, in persuading even the intelligent reading public that it would be well worth their while to read your writings. I shall need the help of my publicity agent, Edgar Marsden. He can work wonders.'

A waiter Stephen hadn't seen before arrived now with two menus. (The high-class Elzivir Club, regardless of the current economic 'recession', evidently hadn't stooped to reducing the number of staff it employed.) This waiter asked Sir Barnard and Stephen which out of the eight listed items they would like for their sweet course.

'Well, what's your choice?' Sir Barnard asked Stephen.

'Dutch apple pie, please,' Stephen said. He supposed that unlike several of the other items it wouldn't contain cream, which sometimes disagreed with him.

'*Dutch* apple pie,' Sir Barnard said; 'that's a very appropriate choice to make in the *Elzivir* Club. But I'll have the sherry trifle.'

After the waiter had gone to fetch what they'd ordered, Sir Barnard said, 'Edgar, my publicity agent, is adept at working out precisely the type of advertisement best suited to each individual author he advertises for me, and I don't doubt he'll succeed not only in making your writings acceptable but even in creating a wide demand for them, though you may find his methods a bit startling.'

Stephen couldn't quickly think of what to say to this, but he tried to look grateful.

'There is really nothing to be alarmed about,' Sir Barnard added, detecting an uneasiness in Stephen.

Before either of them had said anything further the waiter brought the Dutch apple pie and the sherry trifle to their table. Immediately after he'd left them the wine waiter came with a bottle of White Burgundy and two extra glasses. As previously when bringing the Crozes-Hermitage he now tipped a small quantity of the Burgundy into Sir Barnard's glass first, and only on getting a nod of approval from Sir Barnard did he pour wine into Stephen's glass. At this moment Sir Barnard noticed, with a look of irritated surprise, that there was still quite a quantity of the Crozes-Hermitage left in Stephen's other glass. Stephen, who had been feeling that he'd already drunk more than enough, was intending to abandon the rest of the Crozes-Hermitage, but in the hope of placating Sir Barnard he quickly drank it off, and before starting to eat the Dutch apple pie he also drank some of the White Burgundy.

Sir Barnard, who was placated now, said, 'Edgar always takes one of these small new portable phones about with him so that he and his clients can keep in touch wherever he goes. After lunch I'll phone him from the Club.'

While he consumed the sherry trifle, Sir Barnard went on to tell Stephen, 'I daresay Edgar will introduce you to his fellow director, Sheila Kimpton. A remarkable young woman. You may have seen, in magazines and on the box, photographs of her wearing the latest fashionable clothes and attending fashionable events like Ascot or Cowes Week.'

'I'm afraid I haven't,' Stephen said.

'Well, it doesn't matter,' Sir Barnard said. 'In the photographs Edgar and she may ask the photographer to take of her together with you, it is improbable that she will be wearing such up-market garments, but I'm sure they will be suited to the occasion.'

Luckily Sir Barnard without waiting for any comments from Stephen, who was feeling uneasy again, called one of the waiters to the table and told him to bring coffee for them to the lounge when they'd finished their sweet course.

Before they both stood up from the table Sir Barnard had drunk two glasses of the White Burgundy, and so had Stephen, but only Stephen staggered at all as they made their way into the lounge and towards the red plush chairs they had previously occupied. He managed to reach his chair safely, and immediately afterwards the waiter appeared balancing with one hand a silver tray which had a coffee pot and two cups and two small jugs on it, while with the other hand he placed a mother-of-pearl-inlaid coffee table in front of their chairs. It seemed that in no time Sir Barnard finished his coffee, got up to go to the phone and was back again saying to Stephen, 'Edgar will be here within a few minutes.'

Edgar Marsden, freelance specialist in publicity work for publishers, made an ambivalent impression on Stephen as he came briskly towards the chairs in which Stephen and Sir Barnard were sitting. His smile was amiable enough when Sir Barnard introduced them, but he had the sleeked-back black hair and the too smart grey suit that Stephen, quite irrationally, associated with confidence tricksters.

'We may as well go to the studio at once,' Marsden suggested; 'I've got the car waiting outside.'

'I'll see you here again in the Club for tea, I hope,' Sir Barnard affably said; and Marsden, without giving Stephen time to think of any sensible reply he could make to this, glanced at him in the evident expectation that he would now stand up from his chair.

Stephen failed to avoid staggering as he stood up, though without actually overbalancing, and Marsden was able to give an almost convincing appearance of not having noticed that he had been in the least unsteady. As Stephen stepped with Marsden at his side out of the Club into the mild open air of the afternoon, the thought came to him that Sir Barnard might have deliberately aimed to get him drunk and that Marsden might have conspiratorially instigated him to do so.

It did not take long for Marsden, driving his car fairly fast and with Stephen securely safety-belted on the seat beside him, to arrive at the photographer's studio. He helped Stephen to release himself from the safety-belt, and he opened the car door for him to step out, but he didn't have to help him to stand up. Stephen, much to his own surprise, was able to do this without staggering at all; and he remained steadily standing while Marsden went round to lock the driver's door and then returned to lock the door Stephen had stepped out from. Now came the difficulty for Stephen of moving forward towards the entrance of the studio without tottering. But, slightly vertiginous though he felt, he managed to reach the studio door without any help from Marsden.

The inside of the studio was apparently bare except for one single piece of furniture, a large sofa. This was fortunate, because his successful effort to keep steady so far had exhausted him and now he toppled forward and was only just able to reach the sofa in time to save himself from falling to the floor. He sat heavily down on the sofa, into which he sank so deeply that he couldn't imagine how he would ever be capable of getting himself up from it again.

Stephen became aware that Marsden seemed to have disappeared, and that he himself was all alone in the studio. But he was not alone here for long. Two curtains above the dais a few yards in front of him were abruptly parted, and a beautiful woman stepped forward and stood still awhile as if for applause from a theatre audience. She was naked, except for a silkily pink bikini and a small silkily pink mask with two oval apertures through which her dark brown eyes looked directly at him. All at once she leapt across the space between her and the sofa, and she flung herself across his lap and curled one of her arms around his neck. He saw that her breasts were of the rare shape which he found uniquely appealing: she was full-breasted, and because of this her breasts drooped a little, but their nipples pointed stiffly up. He was abandoning himself to a feeling of extreme pleasure when, suddenly, there was a flash of bright white light and he realised that he and she were being photographed. He became immediately sober. He pushed her off his lap and he was able with angry ease to lift himself out of the deep sofa.

Marsden reappeared from wherever it was he had been concealed. Stephen spoke to him with controlled fury: 'I suppose you think that the photograph which has just been taken will help to persuade the intelligent public to read my writings?'

'Certainly I do,' Marsden said firmly. 'This photograph will put an end for ever to the idea people unfortunately have that you are boringly old-fashioned and overserious. They will think of you as a bit of a dog, and there will be a great demand for your books.'

'But the serious readers who already read me and whose judgement I respect will be disgusted with me and will never again be able to think as well of my writings as they previously did,' Stephen said, and then he released the fury he had been controlling and he told Marsden, 'You have behaved like a blackmailing trickster.'

'Very well, if you are determined to act against your own interests, I will ask the photographer to destroy the photograph, and I'm sure my business partner Sheila Kimpton will support me in this.' He glanced towards the masked and bikinied woman who had come to stand beside him.

'Yes, of course,' she said.

Stephen turned on her and said, 'Am I right in guessing that your reason for wearing your absurd little mask was to avoid being recognised by any of your fashionable Ascot and Cowes clients who might see the photograph?'

She did not answer him.

As he moved, perfectly steadily, towards the door of the studio he said to her and to Marsden, 'You are really little better than prostitutes, the pair of you.'

He walked out of the studio and then vigorously in a random direction along the pavement. Within a minute or two, after passing various fashionable shops, he came upon a bookshop, and he was surprised to see that among the books displayed in the window there seemed to be few of the usual best sellers. He went inside. Soon a pleasant-faced young man approached him, and said with a smile, 'Perhaps you don't recognise me, Mr Highwood.'

Stephen looked closely at him and did begin to recognise him, but without being able to remember his name or where they'd met before, though he did remember having liked him.

'I almost recognise you,' Stephen told him.

'I'm Paul Irlam,' the young man said. 'I met you in that famous Continental resort where I took you to the exhibition of paintings by the Excrementalist artists.'

Now in an instant Stephen vividly remembered what had happened there, and he said, 'Yes, you were arrested and man-handled in a police raid, and that was the last I saw of you.'

'They let me out again the next morning, of course,' Paul said. 'The authorities didn't want to frighten off tourists who regarded these artists as one of the main attractions of the resort. The occasional police raid was intended just as a warning to the artists not to go *too* far.'

'Didn't you tell me you were a university lecturer getting material for a book about the resort?'

'I did,' Paul said. 'You are remembering everything at last. And I'm still a lecturer in sociology, though now at a college in this metropolis, not in Yorkshire. I've just been looking around this shop for any new books they might have about the present situation in Ireland, which is the subject I am lecturing on this term.'

'Rather a delicate subject, isn't it?'

'It certainly is,' Paul said. 'I have to give the appearance of being completely impartial, though always hoping that a sublim-inal nuance in the tone of my impartiality will help to slant the ideas of my students in a "progressive" direction.'

'Very interesting,' Stephen said.

'By the way,' Paul said, 'my students are holding a meeting this afternoon on the present Irish crisis, and they will expect me to be there. In fact it's just about due to start. Would you like to come with me?'

'Yes.' But suddenly Stephen felt tired.

Paul evidently noticed this. 'The Students' Union Hall where the meeting is being held is almost next door to this bookshop,' he told Stephen.

'All right,' Stephen said.

The Hall was quite capacious and the audience occupied more than half of the available chairs. Paul and Stephen sat at the back. On a platform in front of the audience the Chairman sat behind a long table with two speakers on either side of him, only one of them a woman. The Chairman asked for questions from the audience, and he got them. Neither the questions nor

40

the answers were of any interest to Stephen, who had heard all of them all too often before. He felt drowsier and drowsier. Then, with the suddenness of an electric shock, rage arose in him and he stood up and, in a voice as loud as he could make it, he told the Chairman and the speakers on the platform, 'Not one of you has had the courage to mention the only possible solution to Ireland's problem – the British must get out.'

There was a silence, and Stephen did not wait for it to be broken. With a brief friendly wave of goodbye to Paul he made his way quickly out into the street.

Walking among the sparse crowd there he began after a while to suspect that he was being followed. This became a certainty when two young men overtook him and turned to bar his way. They raised their right arms and struck down at him with the lumpy grey objects, probably large stones, which they held in their hands. After that he knew nothing more.

Into the Dark

It was the third day since the elderly writer, Stephen Highwood, had been brought to this hospital after being mugged in the street. His wife had already visited him on each of the first two days, and she had become tearful when she had seen him restless in his hospital bed with his eyes half open, and had heard his incoherent attempts to speak. She had said to the house surgeon standing beside her that she felt sure her husband recognised her, and the house surgeon hadn't the heart to let her know how unlikely he thought this was. He'd been glad on her second visit to be able to give her the news that her husband had spoken at least two intelligible words – 'The Pavilion' – but when he'd asked her whether these meant anything to her she'd answered that unfortunately they did not. Now he could tell her that since her second visit her husband had spoken more often and much more clearly than before, saying such things as 'you were a police cadet' and 'they saw in each of their faces a sublime bliss.' Did these refer to anything she remembered? 'No,' she said. 'He was probably dreaming. Stephen often had very strange dreams which he described to me at breakfast.'

Stephen, however, had no doubt that under a thickly clouded sky he was walking along a valley road on each side of which were hills of varying shapes and colours – some rounded and vividly green or barrenly brown, some pyramidal and palely sandy, some tall and sharply craggy, some tree-covered. But nowhere, so far as he could see, did their altitudes seem truly mountainous. He was trying to guess what country he might be

42

in when he heard a car coming up from behind him. It soon passed him, and then abruptly stopped. The car was a large apparently armour-plated one painted over with a camouflage pattern resembling that of a soldier's flak-jacket, and as he approached it a flak-jacketed man aged forty or so stepped down from it and spoke smilingly to him.

'Stephen Highwood, what are you doing here?'

Stephen, who had no idea yet why he was here, evaded the question by saying, 'I recognise your face very well, and your name is on the tip of my tongue but I just can't quite remember it.'

'Dig Harknell.'

'Of course.' Then Stephen quickly asked, hoping he would be able to think up a convincing explanation of his own presence here by the time Dig had answered him, 'And what are you yourself doing here?'

'I am a freelance journalist and at present I'm acting as a correspondent for THE PLANET, the only British daily paper that takes the side of the Rebels against their Government.'

'As for me,' Stephen said, having suddenly thought of a plausible explanation, 'I'm here because being a writer independent of any newspaper I feel I ought to see for myself what's happening and to give a truthful report of it.'

'I assume your sympathies are with the Rebels?'

'Certainly,' Stephen risked saying.

'Then jump into this car. The Government have air superiority and one of their planes might be overhead at any moment and spot us before we can get into the comparative safety of the Rebel-held town a mile ahead.'

As the armoured car bumpily continued its journey, Stephen asked, 'Where were you coming from when you overtook me?'

'On my suggestion we had been reconnoitring in a hilly afforested area six or seven miles back from here for any signs of the enemy's land forces, but we didn't find any,' Dig said. 'I shall do better later, when I've been a little longer in this part of the world.'

'I expect you have been in many different parts of the world since we last met.'

'Yes, I have. I'll tell you about them when I get the chance.'

'And before we first met and became friendly you had already been to quite a number of places.'

'That's true.'

'There's something I've known for a long while and have avoided asking you about,' Stephen said; 'but I want to ask you about it now because there seems a possibility that one or both of us may get killed in this civil war. Why did you never tell me that as a young man you became a police cadet?'

Dig, lowering his voice presumably to prevent the driver from overhearing, said, 'You're well aware you've always had a tendency to suffer from paranoia – you admit it frankly enough in your writings – and I didn't want you to suspect that I am a spy of some kind.'

Stephen could not reveal that this was what he had in fact suspected even before discovering that Dig had been a police cadet, and that he still suspected it now. So he merely remarked, 'I see.'

Dig gave Stephen a momentarily unfriendly glance, as though guessing what had been going on in his mind. However, he said agreeably enough, 'I'll arrange for you to have a room in the hotel where all the journalists are staying. No doubt you'll have money on you to pay the bill, though you do seem to travel extraordinarily baggage-free.'

Stephen slipped his hand as casually as possible beneath his overcoat – he thanked goodness that he was wearing an overcoat in this not too warm weather – and he felt a note-filled wallet inside a pocket of his jacket.

'Yes,' he said, 'I haven't forgotten to bring money.'

Quite soon the armoured car reached the outskirts of the Rebel-held town and was stopped by a sentry. The driver showed him the papers he asked to see, and the car was allowed to go on towards the hotel.

A group of men stood drinking at a bar in the lounge of the hotel as Dig and Stephen entered from the street. 'They are all journalists,' Dig told him. 'I'll introduce you to them, and then I'll go off to arrange for you to have a room to sleep in tonight.'

It became obvious to Stephen, when Dig had introduced him and had left him alone with them, that none of them had heard of him as a writer. He felt depressed by this, and only briefly a little less so on realising that he must be fifty years older than most of them. To have been totally forgotten after a mere fifty years did seem to mean that any fame he'd once had – never widespread – had not deserved to be much less ephemeral than the present wide popularity of journalists like these would certainly be. However, as often before when similar despondent thoughts had come upon him, he was able to find some consolation in the idea that it was the left revolutionary line of his writings which had caused him to be neglected, and that a day would yet come – probably not in his lifetime – when they would be remembered.

This sequence of thoughts was abruptly blasted out of his mind by numerous crashingly loud explosions in the town and quite near to the hotel. 'The bombardment has started again,' one of the journalists told Stephen; 'we get it at deliberately irregular intervals throughout the day. Government bomber planes.'

'Hasn't the hotel been harmed at all yet?' Stephen asked.

'A couple of windows broken during one of the raids, that's all.'

Another of the journalists said, 'It seems that the Government wants to avoid antagonising us too much. They may even hope to win some of us over to join those of our profession who are already safely installed in the best hotel in the Government-held Capital.'

'The Government is far too crude in its propagandising to convince anyone not half-witted,' a third journalist said. 'It claims it has the support of the great majority of the people of this country, and that the Rebels are only a small criminal minority – whereas the evident fact is that most of the population consists of peasants who almost unanimously support the Rebels and have already captured several towns besides this one.'

A fourth journalist said, 'It's time we got out into the town to see the damage before the next raid starts.'

The others agreed, and after finishing their drinks they made their way with Stephen among them out into the street. He had become so unaccustomed – except indirectly and selectively on television – to sights such as he soon saw, that for a short while

45

they seemed unreal to him. Then in an instant the horror of the blood-splashed pavements, the crushed heads, the separated limbs, the severely injured children, struck fully into him. Stretcher-bearers had begun to arrive, and they were carrying away at the run those among the bodies in which signs of life remained. A journalist standing beside Stephen said, 'The main hospital has already been destroyed – specially targeted by the bomber planes, I don't doubt, though of course the Government would deny it. Church halls are being used as makeshift hospitals, and the equipment available there for treatment of the injured is far from adequate, as you can imagine. The best that we as journalists can do to help is to report accurately what we have seen.'

'Haven't the telephone lines been cut?' Stephen asked.

'No; we assume the Government must have decided that it would be more useful to tap them.'

The journalists returned to their hotel, and Stephen with them.

In the lounge, Dig Harknell met him and drew him aside.

'I'm afraid that all the rooms in this hotel are already booked,' Dig told him, 'but I'm pretty sure you could be accommodated in The Alma Hotel next door to this.'

'Then you haven't actually booked a room for me there?'

'I could hardly do that. I don't know whether you would like the place, or whether you mightn't think its charges excessive.'

'Isn't there any other hotel I could try in this town?'

'No; the few others have all been bombed. The Alma is sufficiently close to ours to have been spared.'

'So unless I am to sleep on the street I seem to be left with no alternative to spending a night at The Alma,' Stephen said, 'however dislikable or expensive it may be.'

His tone did not try to hide the resentment that Dig's failure to book him a room there had made him feel.

Without any reply and with undisguised unfriendliness Dig turned away from him and went to join the other journalists.

Stephen had no difficulty in finding The Alma. Even though the light from the thickly clouded sky was beginning to fade, the name of the hotel was vividly visible in brilliantly red lettering above the main doorway. And every paintable surface over the entire front of the building was lurid with clashingly differing colours which almost succeeded in distracting attention from the advanced age and decay of the surfaces that could not be painted.

The front door was ponderous and had metal studs sticking out from it. The doorbell was of the old-fashioned nineteenth-century type that needed to be pulled not pushed. At least six inches of wire cable came out with the decorative bronze knob that Stephen pulled. The door was opened by a strongly-built woman whose face he could not at first clearly see, because of the dimness of the pinkish light in the hall behind her.

'What can I do for you?' she asked, and he could see now that her face was heavily made-up and that though it was not young it might once have been good-looking.

'I would like a room for the night,' he said.

She led him to the back of the hall and to an antique pedestal table with a chair behind it which she carefully sat down on.

'You will have to pay in advance,' she told him; and when he showed surprise she added, 'We find this necessary in these difficult times.'

'How much do I have to pay?'

'Two hundred and fifty pounds, or its equivalent in dollars at the current rate of exchange,' she said, 'and a further charge will be made for any extras you may require.'

'But this is monstrous,' he couldn't restrain himself from exclaiming. 'I can't believe that the hotel next door charges anything like it.'

'You can take the room at the price I've stated or you can leave this hotel immediately,' she said. 'Considering the risk I'm running – you may be a Government spy and I could come under suspicion of knowingly harbouring you – I am offering you the room at a bargain price.'

The thought came to him that if he refused and left The Alma he might be spotted by a Government plane and gunned down.

From the wallet in the inner pocket of his jacket he drew out a wad of English bank notes, and after a careful count he placed the demanded two hundred and fifty pounds on the table in front of her. He was relieved to see that he had at least a few notes left over. She re-counted the notes he had given her, then having made sure that he hadn't cheated her she loudly and a little huskily called out, 'Samantha.'

A young woman whose white-pinafored black dress resembled the uniform of a nineteenth- or early twentieth-century servant-girl, though her hair was dyed bright red and the flesh of her neck was generously exposed, quickly emerged from a door at the far side of the hall.

'Samantha,' the older woman said, 'show Mr —' she paused, and Stephen was tempted for a moment to give a false name but decided he'd be wiser to tell her his real one. After he'd told her she went on, 'show Mr Highwood upstairs to room number three.'

Stephen was not certain whether or not he saw the two women exchange significant glances before Samantha with an impertinent curt beckoning gesture of her hand signalled to him to follow her upstairs.

At the back of one side of the double bed in the bedroom she showed him into there was an open archway which led through to what appeared to him to be an en-suite bathroom. Suddenly while he was feeling the bed to test its softness a naked woman stepped through the archway from the bathroom, and on seeing him she at once screamed the word RAPE and she continued screaming it even after the hotel proprietress – or brothel madame as he now knew she must be – had arrived in the room and gripping him by the arm had shouted, 'Out of this hotel at once. I'm not going to have you lynched on my premises, and lynched you certainly will be when the people of our town hear the screams coming from here and know that you are a rapist.'

She was much stronger than he was and, in spite of his protesting that he hadn't even touched the screamer and was still wearing his overcoat, she forced him downstairs and opening the front door she pushed him so violently out that he tripped and fell almost flat in the street. He was aware of the raised angry voices of people approaching from the town, and with a painful effort he managed to lift himself up and to start walking. A slight hope came to him that the lynchers, seeing him wearing an overcoat, might doubt whether he could be the rapist and would call first at The Alma to make sure that the man they wanted was not still there. He found he was able to walk quite quickly – his fall did not seem to have injured him – and he was helped by a hopeless fear. He knew that the lynchers couldn't fail to catch up with him. And yet as he walked on he heard no sound from them. He heard instead the sound of aeroplane engines overhead. Government bombers must be on their way to raid the town again, and the lynchers had presumably run to take cover.

It was getting darker. The bombers might not spot him on their way back to the Capital and the lynchers might abandon their pursuit of him. He walked quickly on. After a while he saw ahead of him the headlights of an approaching motor vehicle. It stopped, and he noticed that it was a large apparently armour-plated car painted over with a camouflage pattern resembling that of a soldier's flak jacket, and a flak-jacketed man aged forty or so, who however was not Dig Harknell, jumped down from the car and spoke smilingly to him.

'Stephen Highwood, what are you doing here?'

'You know my name,' Stephen evasively answered, 'but I don't know yours, though I do seem to recognise your face.'

'So you ought to. For several years we were next door neighbours in Birmingham before World War Two.'

'Yes, of course, you are Angus Buchan,' Stephen said. 'But how has it happened that you are here now with this armoured car?'

'We are on a mission from the Capital to give an independent report – independent of the one that the bomber pilots will give – of the number of fires started by the raid and how quickly they are being put out. It is suspected that the Rebels have acquired some of the most up-to-date fire-extinguishing equipment.'

'I've gathered from your recent obviously autobiographical book that since our Birmingham days you have visited many different parts of the world,' Stephen said, 'and that you have been acting as an agent for the British Secret Service.'

'You are quite right,' Angus said.

He didn't seem at all disturbed by Stephen's accusing tone of voice, so Stephen went on to ask still more antagonistically, 'And have they sent you to support this Government here against the Rebels?'

49

Angus simply said, 'Get into this vehicle with me and then we can talk at some leisure.'

Stephen allowed himself to be helped up by Angus into the armoured-car and to be guided to an uncomfortable seat beside him there.

The driver manoeuvred the car round in the narrow road to face away from the Rebel-held town and towards the Capital. As he drove on again, Angus said enigmatically, 'He is one of us, so it won't matter how much he may overhear of what we say, though with the engine being as noisy as it is he won't hear much.'

Angus spoke in a very friendly tone. 'I believe that your views aren't any less left-wing now than when we were neighbours in Birmingham,' he continued. 'You do support the Rebels here, don't you?'

'Yes, I do,' Stephen said.

'Now I can tell you something that may surprise you,' Angus said. 'My views are not what they were. I too support the Rebels, and I am acting as a spy for them while continuing to give the Government here and the British Secret Service the impression that I remain fanatically anti-left. I am telling you all this because I have more than one reason for trusting you.'

Stephen did not ask what his reasons were, and Angus went on, 'Tell me why you chose to get away from the Rebel-held town.'

Stephen described how Dig Harknell, who knew he was suspected by Stephen of being a spy, had assured him that there was no unoccupied room in the hotel where he himself and the other journalists were staying, and had suggested that Stephen should try a nearby hotel called The Alma. Stephen next described in detail what had happened to him in The Alma and how he had desperately hurried away from there to escape being lynched as a rapist.

'It is obvious that he wanted to have you killed to prevent you from exposing him as a spy for the Government,' Angus said. 'He may even have convinced the madame that *you* were a spy and a dangerous one who ought to be eliminated. But his plot has been a double failure: you have escaped and I who am regarded

50

by him as a fellow spy for the Government shall make sure that the Rebels get to know of his treachery and give him his full deserts.'

Stephen felt he ought to express gratitude to Angus for this assurance, but at the same time he couldn't help feeling a revulsion against spying in general, even when it favoured his own side.

'Thank you,' he ridiculously said.

Angus smiled, and said, 'I hope you won't mind staying the night free of charge in the magnificent Government hotel where I have been installed.'

'Thank you very much,' Stephen more easily said.

The room he was shown up to by the hotel receptionist had a sham antique bedstead with pillars at its corners and a canopy above it, but the bed itself felt comfortable when he sat down on it for a moment. The receptionist showed no sign of being disconcerted by his lack of baggage. She must have assumed that as he seemed a 'gentleman' and was Mr Buchan's guest, this lack was quite in order.

'Dinner will begin to be served in a quarter of an hour's time,' she told him before she left him by himself in the room. He noticed that the eiderdown over the bed had a pattern of birds and flowers on it. He felt tired, but knew he must not give way to this feeling yet. At the back of the bed there was an archway leading to a bathroom, just as there had been in the brothel. He removed his overcoat and went to the bathroom basin to wash and freshen up his face. He had been wearing a not too untidy suit under his overcoat and he was glad of this as he went downstairs to join Angus in the lounge.

'You are looking better already,' Angus said. 'What about a pre-prandial?'

Stephen asked for a dry sherry and Angus chose a gin and tonic.

The dinner was excellent and so was the claret, but Stephen was beginning to feel tired again and only the fear of seeming bored by what Angus was talking about kept him from dozing off. One of the things – none of them political – which Angus was

51

saying was that the hotel had a really wonderful walled garden, best seen in the early morning of a fine day. But aware of Stephen's drowsiness he before long suggested to him that he might like to go to bed soon and have a sound and well-deserved sleep.

Stephen was glad to take his advice, and was able to rouse himself sufficiently to wish him 'Good night' almost brightly, before going upstairs to the bedroom where the four-poster bed was.

He made a brief very necessary visit to the bathroom to relieve his bladder; then he returned without washing to the bed, which he climbed into after throwing on to a bedside chair everything he was wearing except his underclothes.

Never since his boyhood had he slept so soundly as he did that night. He woke early, and feeling perfectly refreshed he got out of bed and went to draw back one of the bedroom curtains and to look out of the window. In the light of the just risen sun he saw the walled garden looking as wonderful as Angus had said it was. He quickly turned back into the bedroom and going through the arch into the bathroom he first relieved himself, then he stripped himself of his underclothes and thoroughly washed himself all over. He dried himself with the towel provided by the hotel, pulled on his underclothes, returned to the bedroom, got fully dressed in his suit, went downstairs to find his way out into the walled garden. One of the hotel servant-girls, disconcerted for an instant to see that he too was up so early, was willing enough to take him to the door he wanted to find.

As soon as he opened it and stepped out on to a sunlit lawn sparkling with early morning dew, an extraordinary change came over him. He felt that he had become many years younger. He was filled with bliss of a kind he had sometimes experienced in his boyhood, but never since then. And as he walked on towards the wall and saw rising beyond it tall trees which he supposed must belong to a public park there was a sudden deepening of his bliss. A woman who seemed to recognise him was moving towards him, and he knew at once that she was Ellen, who when young had been the first girl he had ever fallen in love with.

'Ellen,' he said, 'how have you got here?'

'Stephen,' she said, 'how have *you* got here?'

'I've come to this Capital town as a writer independent of any newspaper, and I am making an investigation into what is really happening in the present civil war,' Stephen said. 'I stayed last night at the hotel which owns this walled garden.'

'Actually the ownership is shared by the British Consulate next door to the hotel,' she said, 'and I happen to be the wife of the Consul. But you need not look so downcast, Stephen. I have never loved anyone as much as I love you.'

'And I love you, Ellen, and always shall,' Stephen told her, unable to say truthfully that he had never loved anyone else as much. 'I shall love you as long as I live.'

They gazed at each other and saw in each of their faces a sublime bliss.

There was a dark tunnel that led from the walled garden to the public park outside it. Abruptly while the lovers were still gazing at each other two young men came through the tunnel into the garden. They were holding handguns. One of them gripped Stephen's arm, saying, 'You are a Government spy and you have betrayed the Rebel cause.' 'No,' Stephen desperately said, 'Dig Harknell is the Government spy, not me.' 'You are a liar and a traitor,' the second young man said. A gun was pushed hard against Stephen's chest and another against the back of his neck.

He heard nothing as the world around him went into the dark.

A Ship in the Sky

On the fourth day after the street mugging of the elderly writer, Stephen Highwood, the house surgeon at the hospital was able to tell his anxious wife that her husband had made a further improvement since she had seen him on the previous day. Besides being completely coherent still, he had been speaking far more and in much greater detail than ever before.

'And, by the way, he several times spoke a woman's name,' the house surgeon added, and immediately wished he'd not told her this. How could he have been so obtuse as not to realise that the name might be of a rival trying to lure her husband away from her?

'What was the name?' she asked.

He had a momentary temptation to answer, 'I'm ashamed to say I've forgotten', but feeling that this would be unconvincing he told her the truth.

'Rosa,' he said.

'That is my name,' she said, and she was no longer able to hold back her tears.

He considerately waited for a while before asking, 'Would you like me to tell you now some of the other things he said?'

'Yes, I would.'

'I'm sorry I can't remember all of them – there were so many – but one that made a special impression on me was, "I have been forty years a nanny with the same family, and at last I have managed to save enough money to go on this mystery tour of the world before I die."'

'He seems to have been quoting the words of someone's

54

nanny, but I'm fairly sure that in all our married years together he never mentioned such a person to me,' Rosa said.

'Another thing I remember your husband saying was, "What is it that's so scaring about the word 'Andromeda'? I think it must be the hollow sound of that syllable 'drom'."'

'This is just the kind of imaginative conceit Stephen might have come out with in the old days,' she said, 'though I don't think I ever actually heard him say it.'

The house surgeon continued for some time longer to tell her of things her husband had been saying as he lay in the hospital bed, but Rosa continued to be unable to find any clear connection between most of these and what she knew of his real life.

While she and the house surgeon talked at Stephen's bedside he himself was sure that he was walking downhill towards the sea, and that high above the roofs of the houses of a small town ahead of him he saw an exceptionally large ship just on the horizon-line between sea and sky. He was trailing behind him a heavy suitcase with wheels attached to two of its lower corners, and he hadn't yet totally overcome the misgivings he'd felt when receiving two mornings ago a letter congratulating him on having won a free ticket for a voyage round the world in a famous liner. This liner, the letter told him, had been extensively and expensively repaired and refitted, and was now renamed *Andromeda*. To celebrate the occasion of its first voyage as *Andromeda* a number of inhabitants of this seaside town had been randomly chosen to receive free tickets, and he was among the lucky ones. Stephen, who was all too accustomed to get letters through the post telling him he'd won large sums of money, had looked very carefully through the small print of the congratulatory letter to see where the catch was, but he could find none. And now that he was actually on his way towards the ship his remaining misgivings began to be superseded by a growing excitement at the prospect of a voyage which he was certain would provide him with entirely fresh material for his writing.

Soon, as he continued walking downhill, the horizon-line between sea and sky became hidden from him by the town's rising house-roofs. He made his way downward still along several streets to reach the sea front, rightly assuming that a smaller boat would be conveying the voyagers out to *Andromeda* from there.

Moored against the landing-stage at a pier-head was a large motor launch already carrying a number of passengers. A sailor, after beckoning to him to step on board, took hold of his heavy suitcase but clumsily let it slip over the side of the launch into the water, where it instantly sank out of sight.

The sailor quite unapologetically said, 'Well, you didn't really need it.'

Stephen was extremely indignant. 'Of course I needed it,' he shouted; and in his rage he was about to claim that there were things in it which he absolutely couldn't do without on a long sea voyage – but he noticed that he seemed not to have the sympathy of any of the other passengers on the launch, who none of them had suitcases with them.

'Weren't you informed in the letter you were sent,' the sailor calmly asked, 'that everything you could need on the voyage would be provided for you?'

'I don't think I was,' Stephen lamely said.

'You were,' the sailor said, 'and it will be.'

Stephen didn't speak another word during the short time the launch took to reach the liner, from the side of which, quite low down, a gangway was pushed out by members of the crew and was securely roped to the launch by the sailor.

Stephen was the last of the passengers to walk up the gangway. He wanted to have a word with the man who was collecting tickets at the top of it. Fortunately Stephen had not forgotten to bring his own ticket. The collector listened very sympathetically to his complaint about the loss of his suitcase, but assured him it was quite true that everything he needed would be provided for him; then told him, 'Beth Davies will show you to your cabin.'

A white-uniformed pleasantly smiling young woman came forward and asked him to follow her. She led him along an electrically lit corridor till at last she stopped at a door which had the small brass numerals 49 screwed on to it. 'This is your cabin,' she said, as she unlocked the door. He followed her in. She handed him a key, saying, 'And this is your key to your cabin. Now

I'll show you where to find everything else you'll need for the voyage.'

He was amazed by the size of the cabin. Besides several large wardrobes and a very comfortable-looking bed, it also contained a bathroom. She took him into it and pointed out close to the silvery-tapped bath an ample pink towel draped over a rail which she told him was heated. 'A fresh towel will be provided for you every day,' she added. Then she showed him, on a glass-topped table next to a silvery-tapped hand basin, an array of toilet requisites including cellophane-wrapped toothbrushes of several sizes, a loofah, a real sponge, four small flannels of differing colours, and three rolls of lavatory paper – she slid back a door in a corner of the bathroom and revealed a shower and a bidet and also a lavatory pan which had a polished wooden seat instead of the usual cheap and chilly plastic one.

'Now we will take a look at the wardrobes,' she said, and she led him out of the bathroom. He noticed on their way out a yellow towel-like bathgown hanging from a hook on the wall opposite the bath.

The first wardrobe she opened contained dinner-jackets and trousers of various sizes. 'It is thought probable that most of the men will choose to wear them for dinner in the State Room every evening, but of course no objection will be raised to eccentrics who choose not to. When dances are held in the Grand Ballroom the men in general are likely to wear tails and white ties. You can see that this wardrobe contains a selection of various sizes of these tail suits too.'

She moved on to open another wardrobe. 'Here is a selection of casual and formal daytime suits,' she said, 'and very smart and fashionable they are.'

The third wardrobe she showed him contained underwear, even including a dark blue bikini-like minimal cache-sexe that men could wear when bathing in the liner's swimming pool.

'Complete nakedness is absolutely forbidden,' she said. 'And now I must leave you; but if there's anything else you want to know, just ring Reception. As you see, there's a phone – and a phone book – on the table here beside the door. You could also at any time ring anywhere in England you might wish to.'

Then smilingly she went out of the cabin and left him on his own.

He chose first of all to try whether the bed was as comfortable as it looked. He leant on it with both his hands and he decided that its mattress was probably a genuine latex one and that the bed itself was properly sprung, instead of being as springlessly hard as the only beds obtainable in most contemporary furniture shops were. To test it further he took off his shoes and lay down on it with the eiderdown underneath him.

He was wakened by a knocking at his door. It seemed to have been going on for some while. 'Come in,' he was at last able to force himself to say.

A young girl appeared, who could have been in her late teens. 'I am your chambermaid, sir,' she told him. 'Shall I get your bath ready for you, sir, or will you have a shower?'

'What time is it?' he asked her.

'Dinner will be served in about three quarters of an hour from now, sir.'

'Please stop calling me "sir". It makes me feel nervous.'

'I am sorry, sir – I mean I am sorry,' she said, momentarily flustered.

Stephen tactfully changed the subject by asking, 'Is the ship moving? I suppose it must be by now but how does it manage to move so very smoothly?'

'It is gyroscopically controlled,' she said, pronouncing with some uncertainty a word she had perhaps only recently been taught. 'But what about your bath, s–,' she checked herself just in time, 'shall I fill it now?'

'Yes please. Half fill it with hot water, and I'll add as much cold as is needed.'

She did what he asked and then hurried out of the cabin.

As he bathed himself he began to feel bad about the way he had treated her. In calling him 'sir' she was only doing what she had been instructed to do after accepting her present job which she'd assumed to be a reputable one. He had humiliated her by a request that amounted to asking her to be on more familiar terms with him. After all, there were and always had been nasty risks in a chambermaid's job. He remembered a cartoon by

58

Rowlandson showing an ugly night-shirted middle-aged man leaping lecherously from his bed as a nice-looking young girl enters the bedroom. Stephen decided he must think out some way of making amends to his chambermaid.

Drying himself after his bath he wondered whether he might like to be one of those tolerated eccentrics Beth Davis had mentioned who chose not to wear a dinner-jacket for dinner in the State Room; however he realised that this would call attention to himself, which he did not wish to do, so he selected a dinner-jacket of the right size from the wardrobe. But he had difficulty in tying his black bow-tie – ready-tied ties were not provided, presumably because they were regarded as unfashionably vulgar – and he was rather late getting to the State Room.

A waiter approached him as soon as he entered it and led him to a seat beside an elderly woman at one of the tables. She seemed glad of his arrival – the man sitting on the other side of her was preoccupied with another and younger woman – and Stephen was very willing to let her get into conversation with him.

She told him she had been a nanny to the same family for many years and had at last saved up enough money to go on this mystery tour of the world. 'But I became ill,' she said, 'and the mother of the family I'd looked after until they grew up one by one and left home had to look after me. She was getting old herself, quite a bit older than I was, and she felt the burden of it all, but she wouldn't have dreamed of having me put into a home. And then a morning came when I felt suddenly a lot better, and I escaped. I got up early, and made myself some breakfast, and walked out of the house.'

'You didn't say goodbye to her?' he couldn't refrain from asking.

'I didn't' she admitted, 'but I did write to her after I had bought my ticket and other things I would need for this mystery voyage.' He noticed that she was wearing a fashionably low-cut evening dress and that her bosom was unwithered. 'Do you think it was wrong of me to leave her like that?'

'Oh no,' he said. 'It would have been painful for you to tell her to her face that you were leaving her, and to resist her if she had pleaded with you not to go.'

'I do hope that any grief she may feel now I've gone will be less than her relief at no longer having to look after me,' the ex-nanny said.

Stephen, aware that this talk with him was giving her pleasure, dared to ask, 'Did you ever want to marry and have children of your own?'

'I hadn't really begun to think about it while I was looking after her children, and when they grew up and I did begin it was too late.'

'In your place,' Stephen dared further to say, 'I think I should have felt I had sacrificed the best part of my life to a middle-class family who did not value me at my true worth.'

She startled him by saying, 'I shall not die thinking to myself that I have never lived. I know this voyage is going to be an experience for me more wonderful than any that any of them have ever had.'

A strange uneasiness rose in him as she said this. They both became silent, and he became conscious of having finished his meal without being able to remember at all certainly what he had eaten.

They stood up, and as they were leaving the State Room together he asked her whether she would like to go for an exploratory walk round the ship with him.

'I would like to,' she said, 'but I am afraid I would find it rather too tiring just now. I think I'll go to my cabin and get myself ready for bed.'

As they parted in the corridor he said, 'Good night, and I hope I'll meet you again tomorrow.'

'Yes, I hope you will,' she said.

Within minutes he had forgotten all about her. He had gone up several flights of stairs to reach the open deck of the ship, and he was leaning forward over the wooden rail along the side of it to gaze at the remarkably calm moonlit sea. After a while he was aware that a woman had come to lean on the rail quite near to him. She could be in her forties. Her red hair had probably been dyed, and she wore a heavily jewelled necklace in several strands which gave only a few glimpses of the flesh that her low-cut evening gown would otherwise have revealed. She was perfumed, expensively perhaps, but the perfume failed to disguise a rich smell of alcohol.

'What a romantic setting,' she suddenly said, referring he assumed to the moonlit sea.

He didn't like the implication he believed he detected in this, and he commented unromantically that he could not remember having seen the planets Jupiter and Venus together with the moon before now. He added, 'They are the brightest of all the planets. When only one of them is in the sky would you know how to tell whether it was Venus or not?'

'No,' she said.

'The way you could tell,' he said, 'is that if you had any doubt about it at all it wouldn't be Venus.'

'Is that so?' she said, without any pretence of interest.

Then she startled him by asking, 'What is the number of your cabin?'

'Why should you want to know?' he coldly said.

'Well, one reason is that I've been wondering whether some of us passengers have been given numbers corresponding to our ages, – which would be an awful bit of cheek on the part of the tour organisers, – or whether it's just a coincidence that my number is 39, which happens to be exactly my age. Would you object to telling me what your age is?'

'Not in the slightest,' he said, with an indifference that had a trace of contempt in it; 'I am eighty-nine.'

'I can't believe it,' she exclaimed with exaggerated amazement. 'You look at least twenty years younger. Is the number of your cabin 89, by any chance?'

'No it isn't.'

'But you are quite determined not to tell me what your actual number is?'

'Why should I when you refuse to explain why you want to know?' he said.

'I want to know because I want to avoid knocking on the wrong door,' she said. 'Wouldn't you like me to come along and give you a bath tonight?'

'No I would not, thank you very much,' he said; but she looked so deeply insulted that he added, 'Please realise that I'm not rejecting your offer because of any special objection to you personally. I would have refused anyone else who might have made me the offer.' (He hastily restrained a momentary fanciful impulse to add, 'including Venus herself.')

'Would you have refused if your wife had been here and had made the offer?' she asked, and a maliciousness in her tone suggested she was chancing a guess that he had a wife and that he'd come on this tour to escape from her.

Stephen turned his back on the woman and walked quickly away. As he went down the several flights of stairs to reach his cabin an agony of guilt and grief came upon him. Until this moment he had completely forgotten Rosa, the wife he had been living with for over half a century and loved more than any one else in the world. Without a word to her he had abandoned her, his own Rosa who needed him as much as he needed her, and he had started on a tour which was to last at least a year. What would become of her during all that time? No, he could escape from this ship as soon as it reached the first port it was due to stop at, and he would take a plane back home. But though he didn't doubt that when he returned to her she would forgive him, no matter how difficult this might be for her, would things ever be the same between them again? Would she ever again feel able to trust him as wholly as before his present desertion of her?

When he entered his cabin he was attacked by a sudden fear of going mad during the days he would still have to remain confined to this ship until it reached the first port it was making for. He was a little relieved to discover, next to the cellophane-wrapped toothbrushes of several sizes and the array of other toilet requisites on the glass-topped table beside the hand basin, a brown glass bottle labelled SLEEPING TABLETS. Without difficulty he unscrewed the top of the bottle – everything on this ship was made easy, and the top was not of the usual safety type designed to deter children from poisoning themselves – then he recklessly swallowed three of the pills. Their effect was almost instantaneous. He managed to stagger far enough to reach his bed, and to collapse backwards on to it. He was soon lying supinely asleep with his dinner-jacket, trousers and shoes unremoved.

He continued lying there for a while when he woke in the

morning. The idea came to him of a way of keeping sane during the remaining time before he could escape at the ship's first port of call. Till then he would make a point of trying to investigate everything that was happening on board here. The idea appealed to him sufficiently to make him almost eagerly get up and, after shaving and washing, dress himself in the smartly casual clothes he found inside one of the wardrobes. Then he left his cabin and went to have breakfast.

He was not surprised to find how late he was for it. Only three of the other voyagers, sitting separately from each other, were in the State Room when he arrived there. The same waiter who had served him on the previous evening came forward to guide him to the same seat he had occupied then. This was possibly where he was expected to sit for every meal during the rest of the voyage, he thought. The waiter handed him a menu that had an astonishing variety of items on it, including beef and pheasant. Stephen chose what he normally had at home – porridge, milk, wholemeal bread, butter, marmalade and very weak tea. When the waiter returned with all these, Stephen asked whether the lady who'd sat next to him at dinner had already been down for breakfast.

'No, sir. I'm sorry to say she has been taken ill,' the waiter told him. 'If you would like to know more I could direct you after your breakfast to the ship's doctor, Dr Hector Mackenzie.'

Stephen left uneaten on his plate part of the first and all of the second slice of wholemeal bread he had cut, buttered and marmaladed.

Dr Mackenzie, to whose clinic the waiter directed him, was a serious-looking pleasantly ruddy-faced young man, who said when Stephen asked him about the 'elderly lady', 'Are you a relative of hers?'

'No, she was a complete stranger to me before I sat next to her at dinner last night, but I was very interested by the story she told me of her life.'

'She died two hours ago. She ought never to have come on this tour. She was quite unfit for it.'

'I'm sorry,' Stephen genuinely said.

'The organisers of the tour won't be happy about having a

63

death on their ship,' Dr Mackenzie told him, and something in his tone suggested a dislike of the organisers.

'Well, thanks,' Stephen finally and rather inappropriately said before he walked out of the clinic.

As he went back into his cabin to use the lavatory there, he became deeply depressed, and then a sudden terror arose in him again of becoming insane during the time he would still be confined to the ship before it touched port. However, his renewed terror began to subside from the moment when a young man came up to him along the corridor just as he was stepping out from his cabin and was about to walk he didn't know where.

'Mr Stephen Highwood?' the young man said.

'Yes, I am Stephen Highwood.'

'I never thought I would have the luck to meet you on this voyage,' the young man said.

'How did you know who I was?' Stephen asked.

'I've just read your name – and room number – in the list of passengers, and more than once I've seen your photograph in the left-wing press.'

'And why do you think you are lucky to meet me?'

'Because my closest friends and I have always admired you as one of the very few left-wing imaginative writers of literary ability who have not betrayed their principles.'

'I'm afraid your admiration has been misplaced,' Stephen said with shame. 'The truth is I was given a free ticket for this world tour and I was glad to accept it because I thought the voyage would be a long holiday for me which I could confidently expect to provide me with entirely fresh material for my writing.'

Then seeing the disappointment in the young man's face, he added, 'I've already realised how disgracefully thoughtless I was. I abandoned my wife without saying goodbye or telling her a word about where I was going. But I've made up my mind to escape from this ship as soon as it reaches the first port it's due to stop at, and I shall take a plane back home to her.'

'We know from her past letters to the press that she has never ceased to be a left-wing activist, and there is no reason why you yourself shouldn't become one again even before the ship reaches its first port.'

'How could that be possible?' Stephen asked a little sharply, noticing the authoritative tone in which this young man, who had previously expressed such respectful admiration for him, was now speaking to him.

'I wouldn't be wise to begin to give you an explanation while we're continuing to stand in a corridor where other people may pass along and overhear me,' the young man said. 'Could we go into your cabin?'

'Of course,' Stephen said, and showed him into the bedroom in which two armchairs had been provided by the ever thoughtful tour-organisers.

As soon as the young man had sat down he said, 'By the way, what an interesting coincidence it is that the room you've been given is numbered 49. Wasn't 1949 the year when you and your wife finally realised that the British Communist Party you'd so long been members of had ceased to be revolutionary, and you got out of it for good?'

'Yes, you are right. You seem to have a remarkably detailed knowledge of our political lives.'

'I hope this doesn't make you distrustful of me at all,' the young man said, detecting suspicion in Stephen's tone. 'The admiration I and my friends have had of the way you and your wife stuck to your revolutionary left-wing principles in your later years has been our sole reason for wanting to find out as much as we could about your lives.'

'I am grateful to you for your interest in us,' Stephen contritely said. 'Now tell me more about your friends.'

'That is just what I wanted to do. One of the first things I need to make quite clear is that we call ourselves a group, not a party.'

'What is the name of your group?' Stephen asked. 'And for that matter what is your own name?'

'We call ourselves simply The Group, and my name is Kevin Finnimore. There are not many of us in England yet, and we don't advertise ourselves when we take part in progressive anti-capitalist activities here, but our influence is not insignificant, and we have international contacts.'

'It sounds almost as though you are a sort of secret society,' Stephen commented.

'No,' Kevin said, 'we don't hide our name or our aims, but we want above all to be known by our "deeds" – that's to say by our active support for the working-class wherever it is resisting capitalist attack.'

Stephen felt a growing sympathy with Kevin and he was able to overcome a brief new suspicion that The Group might be just another ultra-leftist organisation, and he also overcame the remnants of his earlier feeling that Kevin's tone was too authoritative.

'You must be wondering why I'm on this ship,' Kevin went on.

'I know I ought to have been wondering, but I'm afraid I've been preoccupied with my own situation.'

'Well, I'll tell you. I have been entrusted by The Group in England with a mission to our South American friends who are doing all they can to help the present insurrection.'

'And how are you going to get to them on this ship?' Stephen asked.

'The first port it is due to stop at is within a few miles of the town which is the epicentre of the insurrection. My mission is to bring support to our friends mainly in the form of money we have collected in England and also with the promise that we shall do everything we can to rouse opinion in England against the murderously reactionary Government that the insurrectionary peasants aim to overthrow.'

'How can I give the support you said I could?' Stephen asked.

'By giving me permission to tell our friends that you, a distinguished veteran writer, are wholly on the side of the insurrection, and that they can use your name to gain support from the wavering intellectuals they are trying to win over to the same side.'

'I shall be glad to have my name used in any way that can help,' Stephen said.

'I'm happy about that, and so will The Group be,' Kevin said. 'And now I'd better visit the ship's gymnasium to get some strenuous exercise – hoping it will help to keep me fit for whatever our South American friends may want me to do. After the gym I shall relax in the ship's swimming pool. Would the pool appeal to you?'

'Not really,' Stephen said. 'What I would most like to do would be to see the ship's engine room. When I was a boy I had holidays with my family each summer on an island, which we were ferried to by paddle-steamer. I used to be able to go down and watch with fascination the movement of the two huge glistening steel pistons that drove the paddles. I was also fascinated to watch the engineer, who operated a large lever resembling the levers in railway signalmen's cabins. It could slow down or reverse or accelerate the pistons according to orders from the Captain's bridge conveyed to him on an engine room dial which rang like an exceptionally loud cash-register. The engine room of this super-ship will be very different, and I have to admit I am almost as keen to see it as if I were still a boy.'

'Well,' Kevin said, 'it seems we must go our separate ways, you to the engine room and myself to the gym.'

They came out of Stephen's cabin, and with smiles they parted.

As Stephen descended to the lowest part of the ship he couldn't help feeling a slight trepidation. This was intensified when a tall gaunt-looking man suddenly appeared and challengingly said, 'What can I do for you?'

'I hoped to be able to see the engine room,' Stephen said mildly.

'This is the one part of the ship where passengers are not allowed.'

'Oh, I'm so sorry,' Stephen said very apologetically.

The gaunt man seemed to relent. 'I can't let you see the engine room, but I can tell you something about it and about the ship in general.'

'That's very good of you,' Stephen said.

It was soon clear that this man had become willing to tell Stephen about the ship not so much because he wanted to be nice to Stephen as because the telling enabled him to give vent to bitter feelings that had been accumulating in him about it.

'I am the Chief Engineer on this ship and I know that it should have been put through several more tests before the present tour started. I have serious doubts about the new type of welding that was used to replace the old rivetting when the ship was being renovated and refitted. The steering mechanism too needs rigorous further testing, and I am far from confident about the new turbines. I warned the organisers of the tour about these things, but they ignored my advice. Their only concern was to get their widely advertised world tour started on time. They feared they could lose millions of pounds if it was delayed.'

He abruptly stopped. Then, looking almost menacingly at Stephen, he added, 'Don't repeat anything I've told you to any of the other passengers. It might create a panic. And perhaps a mistaken one. After all, the organisers may get away with the risks they are taking, and the tour could be completed without the slightest mishap.'

Stephen was silent.

'You must on no account repeat anything I've told you,' the Engineer insisted, speaking in an even more threatening tone than before.

'I shall think about it,' Stephen said with dignity.

He turned his back on his would-be intimidator, and walked away from him.

He decided to go to the swimming pool in the hope of finding Kevin there.

Kevin had finished his bathe and had dried and dressed himself by the time Stephen arrived. 'There's something serious I want to talk to you about,' Stephen said to him.

They went to Stephen's cabin and sat in the same armchairs as previously.

Stephen repeated to Kevin in detail what the Chief Engineer had told him, and then Kevin said, 'It seems to me that whether or not the ship survives the whole tour the probability of its failing to reach the first port we're making for is very slight. We must already be quite near there by now.'

Stephen found Kevin's reasoning convincing enough to help him overcome an uneasiness bordering on apprehension that he had been experiencing since his encounter with the Engineer.

'Well,' he said, 'I think I'll go and have lunch now. I feel extraordinarily hungry.'

'I don't,' Kevin said. 'I think I'll wait till a little later.'

With smiles again they parted outside the cabin, and Stephen went into the State Room for his lunch.

He sat in his usual seat, and while waiting for the menu to be brought to him he for the first time took note of the four favoured voyagers who sat at the Captain's table. Two of them were perhaps rich business men who had financed the renovating of this ship, and the other two could be the organisers of this world tour. Their faces were startlingly out-of-the-ordinary, and each face was strikingly different from any of the others. There was one man with an enormous head and tiny mouth and heavily drooping eyelids, another whose head looked as though it had been ironed flat on both sides, a third with a head which seemed almost globular and neckless, and a fourth with huge ears and bulging eyes and a deeply cleft protruding chin.

But Stephen was not able to meditate for long on these heads and faces. A sudden extremely loud ringing sound filled the air of the State Room, and the Captain – an inconspicuously ordinary-looking man – followed by his four table-sharers made their way out, trying unsuccessfully to disguise the need they felt to hurry. In no time almost all the rest of the voyagers left their lunch tables and crowded to get out too.

'Most of them haven't a chance. There aren't half enough life-boats.'

The voice that bitterly said this close to Stephen's ear was the waiter's.

Soon there was a vast scraping sound as of sheets of iron being forced over one another. Stephen knew he hadn't the physical strength even to attempt to escape. The waiter had disappeared. Perhaps he was going to try to save himself by jumping into the sea with a life-belt on. Before very long Stephen noticed that water was visible all over the floor of the State Room. It was rising fast. In an agony of despair he called out, 'Rosa, Rosa.'

Stephen's wife was about to leave his bedside in the hospital on the day of her fourth visit to him there when he suddenly spoke her name. 'Rosa, Rosa,' he said very clearly and in a tone which seemed urgent.

The house surgeon standing at the other side of the bed nodded to her significantly as though to say, 'Didn't I tell you he had been speaking that name?'

Something made her want to test whether Stephen would show any signs of hearing her if she spoke to him. 'Yes darling,' she said, 'I am here.'

To her surprise and delight he answered, 'Oh Rosa, I am so glad.' But then he went on to say, 'Can you ever forgive me?'

'Darling, I have nothing to forgive you for.'

'Yes you have. I can never forgive myself, unless you can forgive me, for leaving you, my dear love, and going for a holiday tour on that ship without even saying goodbye.'

'What ship, darling?'

He did not answer and she could get no further response from him.

But her disappointment was lightened when the house surgeon said with conviction, 'Now we can feel sure that in good time your husband will fully recover and will be able to leave this hospital.'

Fred and Lil

Lil and her husband Fred retired at exactly the same time, she from teaching in a large London Elementary school and he from his job with a small London firm of suitcase manufacturers. Being childless, they could save enough money before their retirement to have a bungalow built to their own specifications in a pleasant part of Surrey; and with her teacher's pension and her lump sum, and with the sum they got from selling their London house, they felt they were well-off when they came to live in their new bungalow home.

The impressive blue-grey fitted carpets they'd bought at a discount from a London wholesaler had been laid a week before they themselves finally arrived in their Ford car, which was driven by Fred and closely followed by the removal van containing the rest of their furnishings. Lil made sure that the removal men carried the furniture to the right rooms – and watched to see that they carried it carefully too, because much of it consisted of loved antiques she had collected over the years. The men worked quickly and expertly and the only problem they had was in convincing her that when a wardrobe, however preciously antique, was too big to be brought through the door or window of the bedroom it was intended for, the usual practice was to saw it in half and reassemble it inside the room. They assured her that the re-join would be invisible, and when she objected that they'd had no difficulty with getting it unsawn through the bedroom door in London they reminded her that her London house was an old one with much bigger doors and windows. She misgivingly agreed to let them do the sawing, but after they'd reassembled

71

the wardrobe she did unreservedly admit that it showed no sign of damage. Remarkably soon they finished bringing in from the van the remaining furniture and the large cardboard boxes containing books and other valued possessions, including indispensable domestic utensils, crockery and tools of various kinds, which Lil and Fred had helped to pack. At last, after waving goodbye to the men and watching the van move off along the bungalow's short gravelled driveway between trees on each side that looked more beautiful today than ever before, Lil and Fred turned to go back into their new home; and as they entered it again they felt an extreme happiness.

For a while they simply strolled around and gazed into every room, delighting particularly in the south-facing windows all with panes of special glass made to let through the sun's ultra-violet rays (which before the Second War were still generally thought to be very beneficial to health and were not yet suspected of being carcinogenic). Next they occupied themselves in finding somewhere suitable in the entrance hallway to hang a large circular mirror and a handsome banjo-shaped oak barometer – wedding presents they had taken with them into their then newly acquired old London house. Also there was a poker-worked inscription on decoratively wavy-edged pale brown wood which wasn't a present but had been bought years ago from a seaside gift-shop by Fred, who liked it well enough to want to see it hanging here as it had hung in their London hallway. The words of the inscription were –

It's easy enough to be cheerful
When life flows on like a song,
But the man worth while
Is the man who can smile
When everything goes dead wrong.

In the bungalow hallway now he gave it pride of place nearest to the thick-paned front-door window where it would get plenty of light, and they decided that the mirror and the barometer should hang on the wall opposite to it. They gave just as much thought to the placing of valued objects elsewhere in the bungalow, but realising suddenly that they both felt hungry they remembered that they hadn't yet unpacked their crockery or saucepans or frying-pan or, more immediately important, the food which they'd brought with them in the car and which was still there. Fred went out of the bungalow to get it; but, while Lil was beginning to unpack the crockery and pans in the excitingly up-to-date kitchen every detail of which she herself had specified to the builder, Fred decided to put the car away in the brick-built garage he was so proud of. He was particularly self-congratulatory about the lockable small safe he had got the builder to construct behind a loose brick removable from the side wall there, and also about the recessed compartment in the end wall where during the previous week he'd installed his lawn mower and other gardening requisites including an old scythe. After checking up that everything in the garage was as it should be he returned with the food to Lil in the kitchen.

She had already laid the kitchen table by the time he came back carrying a large basket loaded with two bottles of milk, a packet of breakfast cereal, eggs, potatoes, tinned peas, brown bread, butter, cheese and bananas. She had not forgotten to unpack the tin-opener, so he was able to contribute to preparing their meal by extracting the peas and pouring them into a small saucepan which he then placed over one of the burners on their new gas cooker; however, he was very soon made to feel that he was getting under Lil's feet, and he went out of the kitchen into the sitting-room to continue unpacking the cardboard boxes.

She called him briskly into the kitchen as soon as the omelette-with-herbs and the peas and the potatoes were ready on the well-heated plates. She had always been a good cook, and this meal, though she had cooked more ambitious meals often before when she'd had a greater variety of ingredients to choose from, was one they would remember for the rest of their lives – just as they would remember so many of even the least outstanding happenings of this first day of their coming into their new home.

They went early to bed in their new wonderfully comfortable bed with bright brass railings at its head and foot, and they had the pleasing fancy that tonight they were beginning their second honeymoon.

*   *   *   *

Next morning soon after breakfast, which Fred did his long-established duty of washing up, Lil set out on foot with a feeling of exploratory eagerness to do some shopping in the village. She found there were two greengrocer's shops but only one grocer's and one butcher's. She decided to test all of them. The two greengrocers were very different from each other in manner and appearance, one of them being small with sleeked-back black hair and a voice and gestures ingratiating to the point of being off-putting, whereas the other was portly, curly-haired and affably loud-voiced. She bought vegetables from both, asking to have them delivered to the bungalow by twelve o'clock, and she was to discover when they punctually arrived that the ingratiating one's green vegetables were fresher than those from the affable one; nevertheless she decided to continue buying the affable one's root vegetables at least. The village butcher she ordered pork chops from was not at all of the jokily jolly ruddy-faced sort she had become so used to in London but was pale and exhausted-looking, almost as if the blood had been drained out of him as it had out of the pig whose carcase he hacked apart with his cleaver. However the chops brought up to the bungalow by his boy riding a bicycle with a large basket in front of it were satis-factorily tender. She took to the village grocer at once. He wore extremely small glasses, had a high-domed bald head, a high-pitched voice and a general air of eccentricity which made it difficult for her not to smile when she ordered the groceries she wanted from him. She was amused too by his young woman assis-tant who was in charge of the wines and who looked nonplussed when she was asked in Lil's best (not very good) French for a bottle of Vin Rosé, but who suddenly understood and corrected Lil: 'Oh, you mean Vinn Rosy.'

When Lil and Fred sat down to lunch in the kitchen she said she'd enjoyed her morning's shopping, and she told him all about it. He too, he was able to tell her, had had an interesting morning. Their nearest neighbour, a middle-aged man who hitherto had exchanged no more than a few amicable words with them during their short busy visits to the bungalow before they retired, had seen him this morning scything the grass that had grown high on the stretch of ground levelled down by the builders for a lawn behind the bungalow. The neighbour had come out into his own garden to speak to him over the dividing fence, introducing himself as Jack Appleby and complimenting him on his scything. After talking for quite a short while they had discovered that the fathers of both of them had worked for farmers, Jack's as a dairyman and Fred's as a shepherd. Each of their fathers had been keen that his children should do better for themselves in life than he'd done. Jack and his several siblings, though the only schooling they got was at the local board school, were all of them able to avoid becoming dairymen or dairymaids, or labourers of any kind for a farmer. He himself had started, and made a success of, a restaurant in a London suburb, and had been able to retire early, leaving his own very capable eldest son in charge of the restaurant. Jack, like Fred, had always wanted to live in the country, provided he could do so as a free man. His one sorrow was that his wife for many years had recently died. He had no wish to marry again, but fortunately for him his unmarried older sister Annie who'd been an office worker in London was glad to retire here with him and was very helpful to him. Lil felt pleased that Fred, always a quiet man who did not go out of his way to make new friends, had so soon found an agreeable neighbour he would get on well with. Now she could with a good conscience spend much of her time away in the village and in the small town beyond it doing many of the things she hoped to do besides shopping.

She didn't take long to begin to make her mark in local life. She joined the village Women's Institute; she offered to be one of the flower arrangers at the village church, and her offer was accepted in spite of her never attending church services – (like Fred she was not at all religious, but she was keen on flower-arranging); she took part in organising treats for impecunious old people; she collected jumble for charitable jumble-sales. She was prominent both charitably and physically. She was a big, rather overbearing woman who readily showed resentment if suggestions of hers were not accepted. A certain amount of not unmalicious amusement was caused in the village by a story going round that on her first visit to the local grocer's she had asked one of the assistants for a bottle of Vin Rosé and had been corrected by the assistant who said 'Oh, you mean Vinn Rosy', and that on a later occasion when with a condescending smile she had asked a different assistant for 'Vinn Rosy', this assistant had answered, 'Oh, do you mean Vin Rosé?' Nevertheless, on the whole the villagers valued the voluntary work she did for them. But when before long the vicar retired, the new vicar's wife informed her coldly that her services as a flower-arranger would no longer be required because in future the arranging would be done solely by Church members. The animosity against the vicar's wife which this snub aroused in Lil was long-lasting and deep. She was full of it each time that Fred's niece Brenda came to visit them from London.

Brenda, now in her twenties and an Elementary school teacher as Lil had been, went almost every weekend for country rambles with Edmund, the young man she had recently married, and on occasional Sundays she would drop in with him to see Uncle Fred and Aunt Lil. Edmund was well-spoken and good-looking, and at his first meeting with them, (which she had given them notice of beforehand), they took an immediate liking to him. Lil, having humorously asked Brenda's permission, gave him a smacking kiss. Then she began at once to tell Brenda of her latest victory in her continuing war with the vicar's wife, while Fred, whose keenest hobby was inventing ingenious gadgets, small and large, soon found in Edmund an interested listener to his talk about these. One invention Fred described which seemed to fascinate Edmund particularly was a Turkish-bath cabinet. Fred had tried making it of wood to start with, but after-wards he'd made a cheaper model with a wire frame. Also, having experimented with a spirit lamp as a means of supplying the necessary heat, he had finally substituted a gas fire. Edmund hesitatingly asked a slightly incredulous question: 'A *portable* gas fire?'

'Of course.' For a moment a doubt came to Fred about Ed-mund's practical commonsense.

'I mean, I was wondering whether the wire frame might have been attached to a fireplace in which there was a fixed gas fire,' Edmund said.

'No. That would have caused too much of the heat to be wasted by escaping at the top and sides,' Fred explained. 'When I sat inside on my stool with the gas fire on,' he continued, 'I didn't know I was sweating till I touched myself; then it was like running a finger down a misty window – it started a stream.'

Fred was about to add that he still used the Turkish-bath cabinet sometimes now since moving from London to the bungalow, but he was diverted from adding this by overhearing Brenda mildly protesting to Lil, 'You really shouldn't have gone to all this trouble for us.'

'Nonsense,' Lil loudly said. 'This is a great occasion, and of course we're going to have a real tea. Come into the kitchen with me, and you can start carrying the plates back into the room now. I'll have our new fast electric kettle boiling in no time, and I'll be using the family's silver teapot to make the tea.'

Fred restrained Edmund, who had stood up with the intention presumably of going out to the kitchen too and helping Brenda bring in the plates. 'That's not your job,' Fred told him, pulling him by the sleeve and getting him to sit down again. Fred returned to the subject of inventions. 'There's a problem about the lid on all teapots,' he said. 'To prevent it from becoming stained it ought to be made to fit over the outside rim of the pot – but that would cause difficulties because of expansion.'

Before Fred could say anything further about this problem, Brenda came into the room carrying plates, cups, knives, forks and spoons on a circular brass tray. He himself, signalling to Edmund to remain sitting, nimbly got up to fetch a folding table and a table-cloth from a corner of the room; then with an apology to Brenda for keeping her standing there holding the heavy tray he quickly opened out the table and spread the cloth over it. He relieved her of the tray and laid the table himself while she went back into the kitchen to help Lil bring in the food and the silver family teapot together with a brown-glazed hot water jug and a blue glass milk jug. Soon they all sat down to eat, and though Lil and Fred both noticed a look of embarrassment on Edmund's face (due no doubt to his forced unhelpfulness), neither of them thought any the less of him for it.

Lil tried to insist that Edmund and Brenda should stay on into the evening, but Brenda said they must catch a train soon or they would be very late indeed in returning to their Norwood flat, and they had to be up early next morning to get punctually to the schools where they taught. Lil as a former teacher understood this and did not press her any further. Fred wondered but did not ask whether they might also be busy tomorrow evening on the left-wing political work which he knew took up so much of Brenda's spare time. Neither he nor Lil disapproved of left-wing socialism – it simply did not attract them much. Their political activity was limited to voting Labour at election times, and events such as the rise of Nazism in Germany and the outbreak of the Spanish Civil War seemed remote to them.

But when Hitler's threat in 1938 to seize the Sudetenland from Czechoslovakia caused France and Britain to mobilize, and war seemed imminent, they could no longer fail to feel serious concern – especially on the day that Brenda, who had been pregnant for several months, came down from London with her mother, Fred's sister Lizzy, to see them. They soon knew that the purpose of this visit was to sound them out about whether they would take Brenda in if the Government decided within the next two or three days to evacuate school children and expectant mothers out of London.

They said they would, but they could not help making it obvious that they were not at all eager to. They even said she could have the baby there if necessary, though their feeling was that it would have been more considerate of Brenda to have tried to find somewhere else to stay rather than in their bungalow. She should have realised how difficult they would find it at their age to adapt themselves to any such upset in their normal routine, particularly as Lil's health had not been very good recently.

They felt relieved but a little guilty to hear from Brenda two days later that she would be going to stay at the house of an old school friend elsewhere in Surrey. However, her evacuation became unnecessary quite soon when Prime Minister Chamberlain signed the Munich pact which ceded Czechoslovakia's Sudetenland to Hitler and ended the immediate war threat. Fred and Lil were glad to hear from Lizzy that Brenda would be remaining in her and Edmund's newly acquired London suburban maisonette, and that together with Edmund, who no longer had to expect to be evacuated with his school at any moment, she could look for a local nursing-home that would take her in when her time came.

*   *   *   *

A few months after the birth of their first child, Wilfred, she and Edmund brought him down to the bungalow to be seen by Lil and Fred, who were pleased – not so much because they were interested to see the baby as because Brenda's bringing it here showed she bore them no ill will for not having been eager to take her in during the Munich crisis.

They got no news from or about her for a while after the German army invaded Poland and Chamberlain declared war against Germany; however, eventually they heard from Lizzy that at the beginning of the crisis leading up to the declaration of war Brenda and Edmund with Wilfred, then a year old, were on holiday in the south coast home of a Headmaster and his family who were temporarily away on holiday themselves. Edmund had to go back at once to London where preparations were being made for evacuating his school, but luckily the holidaying family after returning home were willing that Brenda and Wilfred should stay on there until Edmund found a house where they could rejoin him in whatever county he was evacuated to. Lizzy sent Lil the address of the south coast house where Brenda was continuing to stay, and Lil wrote to Brenda – (it seems generally true that related families would seldom if ever hear from one another but for the women). Brenda did not answer, and Lil might have felt offended if Lizzy hadn't soon let her know that Brenda had moved to a house Edmund had found in the Kentish village to which he and his school had been evacuated. Lil wrote to them both there, but once again got no answer, and she would have finally given up writing to them if Lizzy hadn't written to tell her that the young airman owner of the house wanted it back because he'd been posted to a nearby aerodrome, and therefore they'd had to move to yet another house. Lizzy also told her the news that Brenda was pregnant again. So for a third time Lil wrote. But by now in Kent the 'Battle of Britain' had broken out

79

overhead with frequent air-raid alarms by day and by night, and Lizzy failed to tell Lil that Edmund had got in touch with friends of his living in Hertfordshire who generously offered to take Brenda and Wilfred into their house, and that soon afterwards Edmund and his school were evacuated again, this time to Lancashire, where Edmund with difficulty was able at last to find a house in which he could live united with Brenda and Wilfred and six months old Janice. But now when Lizzy wrote to let Lil know about this reunion she had a letter back from Fred to say that Lil was dead.

Brenda and Edmund, when they heard from her mother of Lil's death, sent a letter of sympathy to Fred, which he did not write to thank them for. He hadn't yet forgiven Brenda for neglecting to answer any of Lil's letters to her and Edmund. He understood well enough how preoccupied she must have been in coping with her two children during all the difficulties and changes of place the war had imposed on her, but he felt she could have found time to write to Lil if she had had the imagination to guess the suffering that Lil – whose illness she knew of – might be going through. And he didn't doubt that in spite of the letter of sympathy Brenda and Edmund had now sent him they were incapable of imagining just what the loss of Lil meant to him.

His practical bent enabled him fortunately to do all that was necessary to keep himself adequately fed, and the activity of cooking and shopping helped to make the grief of his loss more bearable. He had offers of help from Annie, the unmarried sister of his nearest neighbour Jack Appleby, but he declined them. As not seldom happens with ageing widowers he was developing a tendency to be groundlessly suspicious, and Jack who liked him very much was sad about this.

However, Fred no longer felt any resentment against Brenda and Edmund, and he might have felt none even if it had been possible for him to suspect that their visits to him after the war were motivated partly by a hope of influencing him to bequeath his bungalow to them. He wished he'd been able to bequeath it to them, because he liked both of them and their two children. But the loss after Lil's death of the quite considerable pension she had been receiving for forty years' work as a teacher caused him to decide he would accept an offer made to him by Peter Wilton, a younger man than himself who had worked for the same suitcase manufacturing firm as he had: by a legally drawn-up agreement Wilton undertook to provide Fred during the rest of his life-time with an income slightly more than he'd received while Lil had been alive, and in return Wilton would gain full possession of the bungalow and its garage and garden after Fred died. Fred had told Brenda and Edmund about this agreement, and had shown his confident liking for Edmund by asking him to act as executor of his will. He wasn't unaware that his nephew Tom, Brenda's brother, was more practically minded than Edmund and might perhaps be more conscientiously efficient as an executor, but Tom had no car and visited the bungalow less frequently after the war than Edmund and Brenda did, and Fred felt closer to them than to Tom.

He enjoyed seeing them. They gave him the minimum of trouble, arriving with their likeable children in their large second-hand car not before three fifteen in the afternoon, by which time he'd had his after-lunch nap. The children could easily be entertained by being invited to look at illustrated books that Lil had collected for teaching purposes, or they could be trusted to go out and play on their own in the large garden without doing damage to the plants there. He was pleased too that he could interest them in the many pot-plants he had on his sitting-room window-sills, and he was especially pleased once when he was able to startle them by saying sharply 'Mind Your Own Business' before telling them that this was the name of a plant he was showing them. And on another occasion at teatime, which he insisted they should stay for in order to sample the cake he was proud of having made himself, he caused Wilfred to laugh by saying, 'Your father must have cut that piece of cake for you with a small eye.' Also he was gratified that the children liked to be shown some of the latest gadgets he had invented, as for instance the long spills made of twisted newspaper which he'd gummed stiff and kept in a tall vase beside the mantelpiece for use whenever he needed to light the gas fire. Then there was the ingenious means he'd devised for making the pages of *The Reader's Digest*

– a magazine he liked, though he knew that Brenda and Edmund didn't – lie flat when he wanted to read it. He laid it face downwards on a 'bolster', as he named the black piece of iron which he exhibited to the children, and then he hammered it hard, he told them. He admitted to them that there was one problem he hadn't yet been able to solve, and he asked whether they could give him any suggestions. He had found that cotton wool in a cigarette lighter did not absorb enough petrol, and he had tried ordinary wool too but that didn't work either. Wilfred suggested kapok, not really knowing what kapok was, and Fred thanked him and said he would try it. What really surprised Fred was that they listened with what seemed the greatest interest one afternoon when he was expressing his philosophy of life to their parents. 'I've never had a good memory except for making things,' he had told Brenda and Edmund. 'Book-learning – after you've got it you're dissatisfied because there's nothing you can do with it. But if I've once learnt to *make* a thing I never forget knowledge of that sort.'

However there were things Fred would not reveal to Brenda or Edmund except when the children were not present.

He described his life as it was now in his increasingly infirm old age. 'I wake up at five and ask myself which day of the week it is, and I'm not sure; then I get up and look at the almanack, and I'm not sure whether I didn't forget to move on the magnet that marks the date. Only when the daily paper comes am I quite sure.' He also told them that once he had forgotten to switch off his electric underblanket before getting into bed and had fallen asleep on top of it. He was wakened by a burning sensation which caused him to throw himself on to the carpeted bedroom floor. Luckily he was able to switch off the current before the bed was set on fire. But though his fall hadn't injured him he lay on the floor for at least an hour without being able to lift himself up.

As he finished describing this episode to Brenda and Edmund he noticed how alarmed they both looked. 'It won't happen again,' he assured them. 'I have attached a large luggage label to the flex just below where it joins the corner of the blanket, and on the label I've written in capital letters, "SWITCH OFF"' He laughed, adding, 'Of course, if I forget to switch on earlier in the evening I shall find myself with a cold bed to lie in, and old age forgetfulness will have scored yet another victory over me. But if it thinks it has got me beaten it's going to have another think coming to it.' He laughed again, and there was pride in his laugh.

Before Brenda and Edmund next visited him he woke up one morning feeling ill. It might be flu, he thought. He rang up his doctor, Dr Mitcham, who came to see him in the afternoon, took his temperature and told him he hadn't got flu but he wasn't very well and he really ought to have someone else living in the bungalow with him until he got better. It was not good enough for him to have a home-help calling twice a week to do some shopping and keep the place tidy, however much he liked Mrs Larby, his present help (Fred had told Dr Mitcham he did like her and looked forward to her visits). Hadn't he any relative who would be prepared to come and stay with him? Fred mentioned several relatives, including Brenda, who for one reason or other wouldn't be able to come, and he felt inclined to leave it at that; but Dr Mitcham persisted and at last Fred conceded that he could ask his sister Lizzy, who wasn't much younger than he was and rather deafer. 'Write to her,' Dr Mitcham said briskly. Then picking up his black leather medical bag, and saying that he would see Fred again soon, he left the bungalow to visit his next patient.

Lizzy travelled to the bungalow by train and by taxi and arrived tired. Fred produced a cup of tea for her and for himself. Mrs Larby had made up a bed for her in the spare room on the previous day. Lizzy, though still tired, insisted on helping Fred to cook the supper for them both. He couldn't help feeling that her deafness caused her to be as much a hindrance as a help. And as the days passed he grew more and more irritated with her and wasn't able to hide it, and she became very unhappy. She wrote a letter to Brenda which revealed without her directly saying so that she was finding her stay at the bungalow increasingly difficult. Not long afterwards Brenda and Edmund came down from London in their car, and to her joy they told her they had come to take her home.

It so happened that Dr Mitcham was on one of his visits to the bungalow at the time of their arrival. He protested to Brenda that her mother was being very helpful here and there was no need for her to go, but Brenda said that if she remained any longer he would have two patients on his hands instead of one. Dr Mitcham, realising how determined she was to take her mother away, did not persist in objecting, and Lizzy and her brother kissed amicably before she left, neither of them trying to hide the gladness that both felt at her going.

After the bungalow front door had shut behind her and Brenda and Edmund, Fred turned to Dr Mitcham and said, 'You needn't worry about my being on my own now. I have recovered from my illness. I shall be perfectly capable of fending for myself with Mrs Larby to do the shopping for me twice a week, and she'll keep the place tidy.' He said this with such conviction that Dr Mitcham was inclined to believe it, though he decided to ask Mrs Larby at regular intervals how things were.

Fred was able to convince Brenda and Edmund, who motored down to see him a number of times during the months after taking Lizzy away, that he was not only well but actually better than he had yet been since Lil's death. And he reassured them further by telling them that he had made an arrangement with Dr Mitcham that if he became seriously ill he could get help by ringing up Dr Mitcham's house with a pre-agreed brief four-word message at any hour of the day or night.

However, he had a long while yet to live, and Lizzy died several years before he did. But one evening the serious attack came, and he just managed to crawl over the carpet to the phone and to ring Dr Mitcham's house and to give the message: Get me to hospital.

Brenda went to see him in the hospital, but he was semi-conscious and could not recognise her, and she was never able to tell him how much she admired him.

With Alan to the Fair

Most often their double bed was a refuge, but tonight it did not help them to forget soon the television documentary programme about the recent revival of rightist extremism in Europe, West and East, which they had been watching from their sitting-room armchairs half an hour before.

As they lay in bed together Alan said to Elsie, 'And tomorrow I shall be going to the County Council's Seaside Summer Fair where the last thing most of the other people attending are likely to have on their minds – even if they've happened to watch tonight's programme for a minute or two – will be the fanatical faces of those young demonstrators with their obscenely racist banners and placards.'

'No doubt that's true,' Elsie said, 'but the Anti-Nazi Alliance members who will be staffing the ANA literature stall at the Fair will almost all of them have seen the programme and certainly won't have forgotten it. And they will be glad you've been able to come to show your support for them. I wish I could be there too.'

'They know about your arthritis and they won't expect you to be,' he said.

'Probably most of them know,' she agreed; 'and now we had better try to shut that programme right out of our minds if either of us is to have any sleep tonight.'

He put his arms round her, and not much later they did forget the pictures they had seen. Both of them fell fast asleep, but Alan soon woke to discover that only one hour had passed, though he felt he had slept much longer than this. Unfortunately he disturbed Elsie, who was soon as wide awake as he was. 'We could try saying to ourselves over and over again, "I am getting drowsier and drowsier every minute",' Alan suggested. 'That has sometimes worked with us.'

They did try it, and within minutes he was glad to be able to tell from her breathing that she was asleep once more. At last it worked with him also. He had a very long restful sleep. But when he woke he saw that she had not yet woken. Although the time was fairly late in the morning she was sleeping so comfortably that he decided not to disturb her. She was still asleep when he went downstairs to have his breakfast; and when he finished breakfast and went up to look at her once more she was sleeping as deeply as ever. She must need it, he thought, and she won't mind my going off to the Fair without waking her.

He walked down to the esplanade by the shortest route through the town. Even if he hadn't known that the Fair was being held on the large field at the far end of the esplanade, the continuous movement in one direction of crowds of people old and young would have left him in no doubt about where it was. They walked more quickly than he did – though he was going at quite a good pace considering his age – and before long a native of the town, Jerry Appley, who knew him, caught up with him from behind.

'It's good to see you've been able to make it today, young man,' Jerry said.

If some stranger, man or woman, had addressed Alan as 'young man' he would have resented it as an infuriating impertinence, but he had become used to it from Jerry and forgave him.

'You look wonderfully well,' Jerry said.

'I am,' Alan said. 'I'm lucky.'

Jerry had never looked well. His face was pallid, his body too plump. He was a prosperous wholesale grocer who rarely took a holiday, and his sedentary hobby of creating brightly painted statuettes occupied most of his evenings. Alan, noticing that he was carrying a large rucksack on his back, asked him, 'What have you got inside that?'

'Oh, just a selection of my work. Avril Balmforth tells me I oughtn't to hide my light under a bushel and she's sure I could get a good price for my statuettes at the Fair. She'll provide me with a small trestle table to exhibit them on in the Arts and Crafts tent. I'll bet old Councillor Fogarty who so noisily opposed appointing a woman as organiser of the Fair this year will be a bit red-faced now. Just look at the crowds who've arrived already. There's been nothing like it at any of our previous Fairs. People will be here from abroad, she's told me, besides all those coming from many different parts of this country. And to think that if I hadn't been encouraged by her I might not have considered exhibiting my work at all today!'

Jerry's voice towards the end of what he'd been saying at such length in praise of Avril became wheezy. He seemed short of breath.

Alan asked him, 'Will you be showing that statuette you entitled *The Angel* which you once let me see?'

'No,' Jerry said. 'That's too large. Also it's one of my favourites and I'm keeping it in my own private collection.'

I don't wonder, Alan thought. He vividly remembered a half-life-sized statuette of a naked young female with silvery wings and gingery pubic hair whose body was everywhere exposed in intimate detail – except for her feet which were hidden by the gold-brocaded high stiletto-heeled shoes she wore.

'It was a most remarkable piece of work,' Alan said aloud, trying to keep irony out of his voice, and he knew he had been successful when he saw the rather smugly pleased smile on Jerry's face.

They had now arrived behind a short queue at one of the entrances to the field in which the numerous stalls and tents of the Fair had been erected. The entrance consisted of a gap in a wire fence, and two men wearing official badges were collecting money and handing out entry tickets there. Jerry showed one of the officials a card allowing him free entrance as a resident of the town, while Alan having no card was about to buy a ticket when Jerry said to the official, 'Mr Alan Sebrill is a long-established resident. I can vouch for him.' This official then let Alan in free with Jerry, though the other official gave him an unpleasantly suspicious look.

As soon as Alan got into the field he said to Jerry, whose

patronising attitude had begun to irritate him, 'I'm sure you won't need me around while you are arranging your statuettes on the trestle table. I think I'll go and look at the exhibits in some of the other tents before I come back to see yours.'

'All right, but don't be too long or you may find that all mine have been sold!' Jerry confidently said.

Alan left him. Now for the first time he was aware how very many stalls and tents there were here and how dense the crowd already was. It might not be easy for him to locate the ANA stall, which was likely to be a small one.

As he was standing undecided momentarily about what direction to walk in, he had an experience similar to the recently frequent experiences he'd had of suddenly seeing, on one of his afternoon walks down by the sea or up along the cliff path, a man or woman, schoolboy or young girl, who exactly resembled someone he had long ago known well but who, looking just the same age now as then, couldn't possibly be that someone.

A young woman walking directly towards him at this moment resembled so closely the twenty-two-year-old Lara Welbridge he had once been deeply in love with that he had no time to convince himself she could not be Lara before she came up to him and spoke to him.

'At last I've found you,' she said.

She must actually be Lara, he realised, though now he could see that she was not in her early twenties but only amazingly well preserved.

'What made you think I might be at this Fair?' he asked.

'I've known for thirty years that you'd retired somewhere near here,' she said, 'But let's get inside that tent. I don't care for being jostled about by the crowd here.'

The tent she indicated was a big one, more like a marquee, with the words *The Wine Club* displayed in elegantly decorative cursive lettering on a board beside the entrance. Not being members of the club they had to pay – or rather he had to, since Lara did not offer to contribute her share – before being allowed to enter the tent.

The people inside were much less densely crowded than those outside, yet they were much noisier. This may have been due to the wine which, as Alan soon discovered, was free. (However, the drinkers were not allowed to choose the wines they drank but had to take what the bartenders liberally enough served to them.) Alan, believing that inexpensive red wine was likely to be better than inexpensive white, was glad to be given red, which Lara also had. Neither of them said anything again for some time, each of them waiting for the other to speak first. They drank their wine, which tasted to him as if it might have a high alcoholic content, but they neither of them refused the bartender's offer to refill their glasses. In spite of the large size of the tent the atmosphere inside it was very warm, and Lara undid the fastening at the neck of the light coatee she had been wearing. Alan was so startled by the sight of her thinly veiled breasts unsaggingly shapely beneath her milkily white diaphanous dress that he turned his head quickly away for a moment in an attempt to avoid revealing the excitement they had aroused in him. But his face betrayed him.

She took advantage of this, saying, 'How could you have left those last letters of mine to you unanswered?'

'You know very well why.'

'Because your wife would not have liked you to answer them?'

'It's understandable that she wouldn't,' he said, 'and I would have hated to do anything which would have been hurtful to her.'

'How absurd to suspect that I, already a grandmother by then, could have had designs on you. All I wanted was to keep in friendly touch with you. I would have liked to meet her.'

'It isn't true that you had no designs on me.'

'What do you mean?'

'I don't mean that you were scheming to seduce me – only that you wanted to get me into a state of unrequited longing for you once again.'

'You are being offensive,' she said.

'I didn't intend to be. I'm sorry. I just want to tell you what it often seemed like to me when I was in love with you.'

'I don't know what you are talking about. I adored you, and I let you sleep with me. Though of course it had to stop when I married Douglas.'

'There were evenings before that when you purposely got me desperate for you,' he said, 'and then at the last moment you fobbed me off.'

'You're talking like one of those male chauvinist pigs who blame their violence on the provocativeness of women,' she said. 'Not that you were ever violent. You were too effeminate, if anything.'

'Once it was you who used to be sexist. You talked like an antifeminist chauvinist. I remember a favourite phrase of yours – "Women are such bitches". You used it to me when you were carrying on with Douglas and me at the same time, before you married him.'

The bartender was pouring more red wine into their glasses. He looked as if he hadn't overheard anything at all of their conversation, and it was quite possible that because of the extreme loudness of the combined noise made by all the other drinkers he genuinely hadn't. Alan began to feel a slight dizziness which could be due mainly to the wine.

Lara was saying, 'You too were carrying on with someone else while I was carrying on with you as well as Douglas.'

'No, I had had a friendly *faute de mieux* affair with an older woman who wanted to get her own back on a husband who was being unfaithful to her, but I gave it up after I met you. Except once, after several evenings when you had set out to excite me to the limit and then to refuse me.'

'You never needed the least encouragement from me to become bothersomely insistent,' she said.

Alan was goaded on to say, 'But you did encourage me. You knew perfectly well how wildly the sight of the dimpled backs of your knees made me desire you, and that evening you were wearing no stockings and just before I was due to go home you turned away from me and leaned over a low table behind you pretending you wished to move something on it. When the time came for me to leave your flat, and I was about to go out of your door, you were surprised not to see the misery on my face that I had never previously succeeded in hiding after you had disappointed me.'

'You are inventing all this,' she contemptuously said.

'No, I'm not. You decided to come with me to the tube station, suspecting that I might not really be going home. But you saw me buy a ticket and you gave me a disagreeably puzzled look as we said goodbye. You could not know that I had expediently arranged beforehand to stay the night with my older woman friend.'

'You wretched little swine,' she said.

'Oh, Lara, I don't know why I have been saying such mean things to you. I've never forgotten and I'll never forget how wonderful you were to me that summer after I first met you, and all the joys you so happily gave me.'

He could not tell from her look now whether she had been mollified in the least by his contriteness. All at once she stepped away from the bar they had both been leaning on and moved round behind him. He realised that with his back to her he would be quite defenceless against being violently struck by her, and he turned rapidly to face her. She closed with him like a wrestler, catching him off balance and forcing him back against the bar. None of the other drinkers in the tent seemed to take the least notice of this. They could all be as drunk as he and perhaps she too was. The bartenders didn't take any notice either. With one arm round his shoulders she held him close against her breasts, while her free arm roved downwards over him. He was incapable of resisting, and soon he did not want to resist. She began to kiss him, pressing her vigorously moving body against him, rousing in him a pleasure which at every instant was becoming more and more extreme. But so too was a guilty awareness that he was being unfaithful to Elsie.

At last Lara smilingly released him. The sudden thought came to him that what she had just done to him might have been motivated solely by a desire to make him untrue to the wife she was jealous of. He turned abruptly away from her and he stumblingly hurried to get out of the tent, noticing before he reached the exit a young couple embracing, both of them extraordinarily beautiful, with the girl's back against the bar and the boy avidly kissing her. And neither the bartenders nor anyone else among the loudly talkative crowd standing at the bar near the lovers was showing the slightest interest in what they were doing.

Outside the tent the air was not oppressive and he knew he was not drunk. He hadn't had more than three glasses and the wine hadn't been all that strong. Among a denser but less noisy crowd here the thought came to him that he might have wronged Lara in supposing she had been taking her revenge on him. Wasn't it possible that what he'd said about his never forgetting how wonderful she had been to him had revived her love for him and that it was this she had been expressing just now at the bar? He felt a strong urge to go back immediately into the tent and to tell her how sorry he was that he had left her so abruptly. But then he would have to explain why he had done this, and if she wasn't outraged by his explanation what could he say to her next that wouldn't encourage her to expect him to meet her again soon? No, it was impossible, and in any case the dense crowd he had got into outside at this moment was carrying him almost irresistibly forward away from the tent he had left.

The crowd jerked to a stop, and he found himself facing an open-fronted high and wide wooden shed where something was happening which other and taller people nearer to it were partly obstructing his view of. Nevertheless he did manage at last to see a nose-ringed heavy-headed bull being led around by a stout middle-aged farmer. Its name, according to a statement neatly chalked on a blackboard beside the shed, was Fintdave Parader and it was a champion. All at once it copiously defecated on the clean floor; but the farmer resourcefully hooked up to a nail on the wall the leather loop that was attached to its nose-ring, and produced from a dark corner in the background a dustpan and brush to sweep up the excrement, which he then tipped into a shining metal dustbin labelled MANURE. The crowd moved on, satisfied with this performance, and Alan was unable to escape from moving with them.

Very soon they jerked to a stop again, in front now of an impressively big façadeless temporary building filled with brightly coloured new agricultural machinery. This time instead of trying to get a better view he stood firm while the others competitively pressed forward, and before long he was able to slip back out of the crowd and to walk on in search of the ANA stall. But he hadn't got far before he allowed himself to be diverted from his search by the interesting sight of a large wooden construction with an open doorway, above which was a banner inscribed in blue capital letters with the one word OXBRIDGE. Curiosity impelled him to enter it, though he was very conscious that he would be delaying further the offer of help which he had come to this Fair with the special purpose of making to the ANA members at their stall.

The capacious interior he entered now was partitioned into separate sections, each of them appearing to be devoted to a particular aspect of university life. The section which was inescapably the first to call attention to itself was the one with the words *The Beastlies* scrawled on a placard beside it, and with a four-man band playing almost deafeningly loud pop music inside it. He passed this by, and he also passed by the football and the athletics and the rowing and the lacrosse sections until he at last came upon a section that had a bookcase filled with books at the back of it. A short youngish man the surface of whose face had a scruffy appearance as though he hadn't shaved that morning was standing near the bookcase. There seemed to be nobody else here, but there were two chairs in the foreground. The man looked inquiringly at Alan, who civilly though loudly (because the pop music was still very audible here) asked him, 'Would you mind if I sat down for a while?'

'Of course you should sit down,' the man welcomingly and loudly said.

'I'm glad to discover that there are books among the Oxbridge exhibits,' Alan said.

'I think I know what you mean,' the man said. 'The way that the two most famous and ancient English universities are being advertised at this Fair must strike you as strange.'

'Few things surprise me nowadays.'

'I feel that this type of advertising is a necessity if we are to attract able non-Public School students, who are inclined to regard our two universities as "elitist" places where they would not feel at home.'

'I think they may be right about that.'

'So do I, though not all my colleagues among the dons would agree with me. May I ask if you were, or should I say if you are,'

– the man apologetically smiled – 'connected at all with education?'

'Only in the sense that I am a poet,' Alan said, displeased by the man's simperingly facetious apology for reminding him of his age, 'and I hope that some of the young who read my poems will like them and gain something from them.'

'As I have become willy-nilly an advertiser,' the man said, 'I may as well tell you that a large new book of mine has been recently published about modern poetry.' He took out a book from one of the bookshelves behind him.

'May I ask your name?' Alan said.

'Aubrey Marshall.'

'I haven't read your book yet, though I have seen various reviews of it.'

'I hope you will read it.'

'I gather you have included me in it, and not very favourably.'

Marshall looked slightly embarrassed.

'What is your name?' he asked.

'Alan Sebrill. Of course I know that the accounts reviewers give of the books they review are not necessarily accurate.'

'I may have had critical things to say about you, but so I have about other writers. None of the others have been sensitive about my criticisms of them.'

'Nor am I sensitive about your criticisms of me,' Alan said. 'I might be if when I've read your book I come to take the same view of it as some of your critics agree in taking of it.'

'What view?'

'Well, for one thing, they claim to detect in it a sourness towards writers in general.'

'That's quite untrue of my book,' Marshall said, his face showing obvious signs that he was stung by this criticism.

'I hope you won't be offended if I go on to remind you of some of their other criticisms?'

Marshall looked threatening, but he said nothing. Alan went on, 'They say that you attack me in a way that is prejudiced, muddled, inaccurate and unscholarly. They say that in your index you mockingly misname my latest collection of poems, and one of them describes this as the act of a pert and insolent egoist.'

Marshall moved towards him. 'I consider I am fully justified in treating grossly overrated poets with complete contempt,' he said.

Alan stood up from the chair he had been sitting in. 'Whether you're justified or not I won't dispute,' he said, 'though of course you are fully entitled to express your opinions, as the saying goes, and I wouldn't dream of wishing I'd had the power to censor anything you've written about me in your book – not even the arrogantly disparaging statement I've been told you made that my poems would never have been heard of but for the boosting they got from my Public School pals. Did you actually write something like that?'

'I certainly did, and I stand by every word of it.'

'You sound as though you disapprove of English Public Schools, and I would agree with you in that,' Alan said. 'But may I ask if you yourself were a Public School boy? Or were you a Grammar School boy? I think an answer from you on this subject might be of some sociological interest.'

Marshall menacingly moved still closer to him.

'So you would prefer not to answer?'

'Get out of here at once.'

'I shall go when I choose,' Alan said.

Marshall raised both hands as though about to push him backwards towards the doorway.

Alan quickly added, 'If you try using physical force against me I shall resist. No doubt you are stronger than I am and you could overpower me and throw me through the doorway on to the grass outside. But this would be unlikely to improve your perhaps already dubious prospects of academic advancement.'

Marshall stood looking at him with hatred.

Alan said, 'However, we have something important in common which should help us to see this little tiff between us in proportion. We are both of us, in our different ways, victims.' Marshall's look did not change, and Alan went on, 'You are an academic victim. There are of course two main types of academic victim, one type being the conscientious first-rate researcher who has great difficulty getting his or her work adequately funded, and the other being the type who supplements an insufficient

95

income by contributing reviews to various quality newspapers and periodicals, and by the prolific production of flashily written unscholarly books.'

At last Marshall did speak, 'How much longer do you intend to stand here mouthing out your senilely imbecile insults?'

'I shall leave you as soon as I have told you how I too am a victim,' Alan said. 'Whatever you may say, I know that there is real worth in my poetry – though I wouldn't rank myself among the best poets of our century – yet I tend to be neglected because most of my poems are political and, worse still, my political views are contrary to those that are dominant in this country now. I wonder whether your inability to find any literary value in my poetry has been due at least partly to an abhorrence of my politics? Do you comment on my politics in your book at all?'

Marshall did not answer.

Alan said, 'I wish I hadn't allowed myself to be goaded into attacking your book. My normal practice is to ignore hostile critics. It's true that some of them have involuntarily helped me by pointing out faults which I have been glad to correct. But your criticisms, you may not be sorry to know, haven't helped me in the slightest. And I feel I have degraded myself almost to your level by using the kind of sarcasms and indirect vituperation I have used in speaking to you today.'

Alan turned away and walked, without hurrying, towards the exit of the Oxbridge exhibition, half-expecting to hear as he went an outraged following shout from Marshall. But even if Marshall had been unsubtle enough to shout abuse at him Alan would have been prevented from hearing it by the pop music of *The Beastlies* which became overwhelmingly louder as the distance between him and Marshall increased.

The crowd outside was surprisingly not dense, and for an instant he was able to glimpse not far ahead a stall with a long red-lettered ANA pennant undulating in the air from a high pole beside it. With his heart beating hard he walked quickly towards it, but he hadn't got far before a tall hatless middle-aged man with thick grey hair deliberately obstructed him.

'Good afternoon, Mr Sebrill,' the man said, standing directly and smilingly in front of him.

'I'm sorry,' Alan said with cold politeness 'but I don't think I know who you are.'

'I am Varley Cresnor. You taught me in the Sixth Form at Condell's long ago.' The man's voice was friendly. 'I wouldn't expect you to recognise my face after so many years.'

Alan suddenly did recognise it – by the very large white ears which curved back tightly against the sides of Cresnor's head.

'Yes, I do remember your face,' he said, 'and of course I've never forgotten your name, which has become a distinguished one. I suppose you are still working for the Foreign Office?'

'Not exactly,' Cresnor said abruptly, seeming disinclined to explain what this meant.

Alan might have pressed Cresnor for an explanation, but a more immediately interesting question came into his mind.

'And how did you recognise me?' he asked.

'I hope you won't suspect me of trying to flatter you,' Cresnor said, 'but the truth is that you have retained more than a trace of those same good looks you had when you taught English in the Sixth Form.'

Although Alan couldn't help being pleased by this compliment, there was now another question he felt he must ask Cresnor.

'How did you discover I had retired to this district?'

'I occasionally come to visit an elderly aunt of mine who lives here,' Cresnor said, 'and on one of my visits I happened to attend a public meeting organised by that little group I believe you belonged to – Unisoc I think it was called – and you made a short speech there. So you see it wasn't only your good looks that enabled me to recognise you today.'

Cresnor's answer made Alan feel slightly uneasy, though the tone in which it was spoken was respectful and suggested that Cresnor hadn't forgotten he'd once been a pupil of Alan's. Alan was silent.

'Are you intending to go to the ANA stall?' Cresnor startled him by saying.

'Yes, I want to help them sell some of their pamphlets.'

'I hope you won't mind my advising you not to go there. I happen to know that a large number of right-wing extremists from

97

abroad are likely to be there together with a similar lot from this country.'

'How do you *happen* to know?' Alan bluntly asked.

'Through my new job, which as I've already mentioned, is not exactly for the Foreign Office.' Cresnor's tone made quite clear that he wouldn't reveal anything more about this job. Alan wondered if he might be some kind of high-ranking undercover agent employed by one of those state organisations operating without Parliamentary control against any national, or in this case international, political movement considered at any time by the organisation to be subversive.

'Aren't the police prepared to prevent the rightists from using violence?' he asked.

'I take it for granted they are, but this isn't my department.'

'You don't think there's a possibility that they might not be altogether unsympathetic towards right-wing subversives, and that they might even be in no great hurry to intervene if there were an attack on the stall?'

'I can't share the distrustful opinion you seem to have of the police,' Cresnor said.

'Then why did you warn me against helping the ANA to sell pamphlets today?'

'Well,' Cresnor said mildly, 'for one thing because if you do help them you will have to put up with a good deal of hostile shouting from a large crowd around the stall. But also because I would like to dissuade you from continuing to support a movement in which left-wing extremists play a leading part.'

'Left-wing extremists?' Alan said with displeased surprise. 'What do you mean by that?'

'I mean Revolutionaries. People who believe that the existing political and economic system will have to be completely overthrown before any change for the better can be made in our society.'

'The ANA is concerned solely with defeating the neo-Nazis. To imply that its leaders intend to use it for subversive purposes is simply absurd,' Alan said.

'Don't misunderstand me,' Cresnor calmingly said. 'I abominate the Nazis every bit as much as you do. What I'm rather troubled about is the danger that you might get involved once again with a self-declared Revolutionary Party, as you were in the 'thirties.'

Alan was taken aback by this, and several moments passed before he could retort. 'It's true I was slow to recognise that the Party I'd joined had betrayed the principles on which it was founded,' he said, 'but I hope I have learned from my experience then. I shall be watchful for any signs of a similar betrayal now.'

'I'm very glad to hear it,' Cresnor said, 'though I would be even more glad if you decided not to put your trust at all in the Party that leads the ANA.'

'Tell me of any other Party organising effective resistance to the neo-Nazis in this country,' Alan said.

'By which you mean resistance on the streets, I assume.'

'Yes, I do. That's where the Nazis operate, and that's where they can and must be stopped. And that's where they operated in Germany in the 'thirties – successfully, because too many of those Germans who abominated them believed that the best policy was to ignore their street marches.'

'I think you are taking a somewhat over-simplified view of the period,' Cresnor patiently said. 'The situation now is very different indeed. The powers-that-be in the advanced countries today are almost as strongly opposed to right-wing extremism as they are to the left-wing variety.'

'I don't think they would want to suppress neo-Nazism altogether,' Alan said. 'They know that this would strengthen the left, just as the left knows that the "powers-that-be" would be to some extent weakened if the Nazis were driven off the streets.'

'You are evidently quite determined to support the extremist leaders of the ANA,' Cresnor said, mildly still. 'Have you ever considered the kind of effect this is likely to have on you?'

'What kind?'

'The same kind that your loyalty to your Party had on you in the 'thirties. I am thinking of the wrong you did, the harm you did, to your own nature, to your true self.'

'How can you know anything about my "true self", whatever that may mean?' Alan asked, not trying to hide his resentment at the patronising tone he detected in Cresnor's remark.

'Sixth Formers can sometimes have a more acute insight into the characters of their teachers than their teachers themselves have,' Cresnor said, unperturbed. 'We saw you as a sensitive young man quite unsuited to political activity of any kind – not just of the kind that a few of us knew you were actually engaged in. Also we saw you as a poet, and some of us thought that politics is bad for poetry. I still think so.'

'The truth is that left-wing poetry in the 'thirties was admired by most of the intelligent young, if not by you,' Alan said, 'though I would agree that my politics weakened my poetry and finally stopped me writing it for some years. But this was because the Party line I loyally followed went rotten. If the Party hadn't betrayed its principles my loyalty to it would have helped me to write far better poems than if I'd believed as you do that poetry should be a-political.'

'I am still certain that you could have realised yourself best as a poet if you had been much more independent-minded than you ever were,' Cresnor said decisively. 'But enough of all this about poetry. What troubles me most is to know that nothing I have said is likely to dissuade you from offering your help to the ANA at their stall today.' There was a note of almost sad resignation in Cresnor's voice. He went on, 'Well, you must go your own way, and I sincerely wish you good luck. I shall be thinking of you.'

He stood aside to let Alan walk on, but for a moment Alan did not move. Then 'Goodbye', he heard himself say. However, Cresnor said nothing in response, and Alan quickly left him.

Once again, as before being obstructed by Cresnor, Alan was free to approach the unmistakable ANA stall with its red-lettered pennant. But he was surprised that so few people were around the stall, and even more surprised to find only one person inside it. A woman, sixtyish, bright-faced and handsome, who eyed him fixedly and amiably.

'I am someone from your past,' she said smiling. As soon as she spoke he knew who she was, and her name was on the very tip of his tongue when she told him, 'I am Betty Dale.'

He and Elsie had met her in the peace movement years ago

and he had never forgotten her lively cheerfulness then which she still showed in her looks and manner now.

'Of course I remember you,' he said warmly, 'and I am so glad to meet you again. But why have you been left to staff this stall on your own? Where are all the other members of the group?'

'They have gone off to demonstrate against the international neo-Nazis at their stall.'

'Haven't you had any trouble here at all since they went off?'

'Only a brief bit of verbal abuse from one or two of the usual types,' she said. 'The majority who have come to the stall have been well-disposed and I have sold quite a number of our pamphlets.'

He then told her of his encounter with Cresnor.

'I am glad he was mistaken in thinking you would have to put up with hostile shouting from large crowds of Nazis surrounding our stall,' she said. 'We have gone on the offensive against them, and there are many more of us than of them, and we shall have the support of the crowd, who mainly detest them. We shall non-violently bottle them up in their large stall, and not even the police will be able to help them to creep away until we allow it.'

'This is great news,' Alan said.

'Yes, but we must be alert against becoming at all complacent. Even if the ANA does succeed in preventing the Nazis from holding public meetings or marches anywhere in Britain – and I'm sure this can be done – there will be some among them capable of adopting terrorist tactics, perhaps on a large scale.'

'Like exploding a bomb in a crowded railway terminus?'

'It *could* happen,' she said.

'The idea being,' he said, 'that in a world already suffering from deadly pollution and from minor reactionary nationalistic wars which grow steadily bigger and from famine which is killing millions, a massacre perpetuated in one of the comparatively rich countries might give its rulers a pretext for establishing a fascist dictatorship.'

'I think we need to warn ourselves against ever abandoning the ultimate optimism that we as socialists must have,' she said.

Only a moment or two after she'd said this there was a powerful explosion quite close to them. It caught hold of Alan and hurled him up into the air. Yet he retained consciousness and he felt no pain. He was strangely sure that the blast had not injured him, but he was taking an ominously long time to reach the ground again – long enough for him to hope that, whatever happened to him when he did reach it, the explosion had not seriously harmed Betty Dale.

He was just conscious even after hitting the ground. Someone was speaking to him, but it was not Betty. It was Elsie.

'You are going to be very late for the Fair,' she was saying. 'I've got your breakfast ready for you. You can still be in time to help the ANA members at their stall.'